FLUTES *of* DEATH

FLUTES *of* DEATH

Driss Chraïbi

Translated by Robin A. Roosevelt

A Three Continents Book
LYNNE RIENNER PUBLISHERS
BOULDER & LONDON

A *Three Continents Book*

Published in 1997 by
Lynne Rienner Publishers, Inc.
1800 30th Street, Boulder, Colorado 80301

Translated from *Une Enquête au Pays*
© 1981 by Driss Chraïbi, as published by Editions du Seuil, Paris, France
© in translation 1985 by Robin Roosevelt;
    © 1996 by Lynne Rienner Publishers, Inc.
Cover art and drawings by Max K. Winkler © 1985 by Three Continents Press;
    © 1996 by Lynne Rienner Publishers, Inc.
First published in English in 1985 by
Three Continents Press, Inc.

ISBN 0-89410-327-X
Library of Congress number 83-50204

Printed and bound in the United States of America

The paper used in this publication meets the requirements
of the American National Standarrd for Permanence of
Paper for Printed Library Materials Z39.48-1984.

10 9 8 7 6 5 4 3 2

Il suffit qu'un être humain soit là,
sur notre route, au moment voulu,
pour que tout notre destin change.

—D. C.

To Michel Chodkiewicz and
Jean-Marie Borzeix

1

The Chief of Police arrived in the village on a July midday. Between the high plateaus and the escarpment of the Atlas, the sky was white and ablaze with a million suns. The chief was in a small, ordinary car, with no distinctive markings, such as a siren or strobe light on the roof. He was on a secret mission, and he wanted to stay inconspicuous. There was a whole pyramid of chiefs above him, most of whom were nameless. But as far as he was concerned, orders were orders. They flowed down from the top to the bottom of the hierarchy. They reached him in the form of impersonal memos, scrawled in red pencil, followed by an illegible signature. Of course, anyone could go into his office when he wasn't there and leave a scrap of paper on his desk. But the chief obeyed only those notes sealed with the official seal bearing the imperial eagle. He was far from being careless or a fool.

He stopped his car on the pebbly square of the village, cut the ignition, let out a sigh, loosened his damp collar, and jabbed his traveling companion, Inspector Ali, whose head lay quietly on the dashboard.

— Wake up! he bellowed.

The inspector sat up, yawned and gazed at his chief with two sand-filled eyes.

— I wasn't sleeping, chief, he said in a thick voice. By Allah and the Prophet, I was just thinking things over.

— Well, don't, said the chief. It makes me ill. Do you have any aspirin on you?

— No, chief.

— Well, stop thinking. Otherwise your skull will start to ache. Then you'll get a headache and end up with meningitis. Do you know what meningitis is?

The inspector looked bewildered.

5

— Menin-what? No, what is it?

— I'd be happy to inform you, said the chief condescendingly. Listen up: It grabs you like this, sneaks up on you with no warning, in the center of your skull. (To illustrate, the chief placed his index finger on the inspector's head and pressed hard.) And then it begins to spread out towards the temples, like this . . . and then there, towards the forehead, and then down the nape of your neck. It gets hotter and hotter, pfff-pfff, it never stops getting hotter. (For no apparent reason, the chief's voice became suddenly thunderous.) And all of a sudden, your head explodes, like one of those grenades they throw at demonstrators.

The inspector wiped his face with the palm of his hand.

— Chief, you wouldn't have some aspirin, by chance?

— I don't have any, he replied categorically. You've simply got to take precautions before starting to think. Me, I don't think. I carry out orders.

The inspector said nothing. His adam's apple bobbed up and down. His eyes were empty.

— Follow my advice faithfully. Don't think. *Act!* That's the way it is. If you follow my advice, you'll find your place in the sun. Believe me, I wish you well. If I didn't, I wouldn't be your chief. That's obvious.

The inspector, mouth open, nodded his head at each sensible sentence his chief tossed out at him.

— So tell me, what were you thinking about earlier? May we know?

The inspector swallowed his saliva and put on a big smile which stretched from ear to ear. One saw more of his gums than of his teeth.

— Sure, chief, it's very simple, and doesn't take any imagination. It's this: I was saying to myself: If I was the government, in a manner of speaking, you understand . . .

— Of course . . .

— . . . if I was a minister, for example, or a *caid*, or even one of these big-wig capitalists, well, I'd change everything. Pronto!

The chief, all ears, cocked his head and asked:

— *Every*thing? What do you mean by everything?

— The path, of course!

— Oh, really?

— Sure, chief, I meant . . .

— Yes? The chief pulled from his pocket a pencil and an old fat notebook, with a brown cover, held together by a big rubber band. He didn't open the notebook, not yet. With his thumb and forefinger, he distractedly pulled on the rubber band, snapping it against the cover. He didn't even glance at the inspector.

— Yes? he repeated. What did you want to say? Which path?

— It's nothing, chief. Nothing at all. The truth is I fell asleep along the way. I had a bad dream, one of those nightmares, you know. It was the soup.

— What soup? asked the chief suspiciously.

6

— I'm going to explain. Don't get annoyed. This morning, my wife refused to get up and make my breakfast . . . honey cakes, mint tea, the good things in life. It was barely daylight and she was exhausted. So, I had to reheat last night's chick pea soup. Understand?

— No, said the chief.

— It sat in my stomach. The trip was painful. All that shaking around. And on top of it, it was devilishly hot. Two or three minutes later, the inspector said timidly: It is hot, isn't it?

— Hmm, said the chief.

He had pocketed his pencil and began to fan himself absently with the notebook, as though thinking of something. His face was becoming redder and redder.

— I'm sick of hearing about this woman! he burst out finally. Aren't you?

— I . . .

— Divorce, concluded the chief. Repudiate her. Send her packing. Good God, a good for nothing like that who sacks out in bed is worthless to a government functionary like you.

— What about the kids? asked the inspector whose brain appeared to be laboring.

— Obviously you keep them with you. She has no right to them! You are their father. The law is on your side. As your boss, I'll support you.

— Really, chief? Are you married?

— I've gotten rid of two who didn't work out. And I buried a third after two years of marriage. It just shows that women today aren't what they used to be: obedient, hard-working, and all that. They're nothing but poison. Let me tell you, civilization isn't worth a thing. Nowadays, they even need a washing machine!

On and on he went in that vein, dwelling on the lax morals which have a tendency to shuffle backward like a Moroccan donkey; vilifying the movies, the pill, politics; inveighing against the petrol Kings, the Russians; expounding on the world situation in lapidary platitudes. When he had finally vented some of the hot air which had threatened to make him pop, he stopped, caught his breath, and said:

— You never stop arguing! You've got to work! Let's see, now. I'll fix up this notebook. I won't turn in a report on you to my superiors. For a moment, I thought you might be one of those "insectuals." But now I understand. I really do. You are a victim of the matriarchy.

— Yes, chief.

The inspector listened to his boss as though he were in the mosque, taking in every single word, and every little gesture. When he saw the chief's notebook disappear into his pocket, he said:

— Thank you very much, chief. By Allah and the Prophet and the Prince of Believers, Saint Hassaan Tatani, may the souls of your ancestors rest in peace wherever they may be!

— Let's not speak of it anymore, said the chief, suddenly becoming jovial.

Two childish dimples appeared in his big, rosy cheeks.

— What I was saying earlier is pure logic, continued the inspector. My wife still asleep at six in the morning, that old soup sitting in my stomach, the road full of rocks and holes. Everything runs together like dried figs on a string. Like two and three makes five.

— Oh?

— Yes, chief, naturally. If I've got it right, we left the city on a beautiful highway. Pretty soon it turned into a regular two-way road, and finally a single track. So you see? The further we left the government behind and crept towards the hills, the more there was nothing but a dirt road, a mule track with bumps and ruts, scratched up like a chicken yard, full of pebbles and scrubby bushes with thorns as big as this. (He held out his thumb, then his whole hand for good measure.) Well, we're not mules! Especially you chief. You follow me?

— I follow you.

— Hold off on your old notebook, said the inspector suddenly. Leave it where it is.

— Go ahead.

— What I was saying seems obvious to me. I don't know what it's due to, whether the chick peas, my wife with her cold, the nightmare, or what, but I was saying to myself that if I were the government, I'd put everything in good order without a moment's delay. I'd sweep up all these idle people, these kids with their records and guitars, these hippies ...

— Insectuals! People who work with their heads.

— Precisely, chief, all these crazy head-workers. Make them pick up the stones and brambles on this old country track and turn it into a beautiful macadam highway, for the good of the country, and so you can come to this mountain village smoothly and gently, as surely as two and four makes six. Not to mention the reduction in unemployment. Now isn't that a smart idea?

Then he shut up. The chief stayed silent for a long time, carefully watching his subordinate's expressionless face, weighing the pros and cons, sorting out what he had just heard. Goodness, but here were some ideas which he could not only understand, but even accept: ideas which involved him and his world order directly. There were others which didn't fit in at all with his scheme of things, short scraps of ideas without form or substance, like communism on Arab soil. For a long time, he rubbed the back of his neck, trying to crack a cervical vertebrae. Then he said:

— But you're not the government, right?

— No, alas.

— Take back that last word, right away, cried the chief.

— Which one?

— The last one you said.

— I take it back, said the inspector.

He took out a big checked handkerchief and spat into it. The offensive word, no doubt.

— That's fine, complained the chief. Don't start up again. He pushed his head forward, stretched his neck, and a bone cracked.

— Got it! That vertebrae is finally unjammed. He began dutifully to crack his knuckles, slowly, carefully, as though he were keeping time. Joint after joint. With each crack, the inspector jumped in his seat. The chief's fingers were pudgy and hairy, his hands short and thick.

— You don't know anyone in government to share your nice idea with, do you?

— No chief, no one, as sure as two and five make . . . how much is that?

— Seven. You don't know any of the police chiefs who could say a word or two to affect the government?

— No one, chief, except you.

— Well, then, listen well to your chief who's speaking to you here and now, in flesh and blood. Stop babbling and listen up: You've got degrees, if I've read you dossier right?

— Yes, chief, the Study Certificate. I got it when I was thirteen with no problem.

— It's a good diploma! Me, I've got a "brevet" degree, obviously. You've got nothing else?

— Oh, yes, cried the inspector with a big smile. I was right wing on the Settat soccer team. I got fourteen goals, me alone, in one season. If I hadn't joined the police force, I could have been playing in the Morocco-Yugoslavia match next Sunday. I don't agree with the choices. Why did they do away with Maati? He's a dynamite scorer. Maybe he's too political?

— Take this thumb, said the chief.

— Which one?

— The one I'm holding out, you imbecile. I don't have thirty-six of them.

The inspector grasped the thumb with a strong hand and waited for orders.

— I'm going to count. At three, give a good pull and crack it.

— Understood, chief.

— Watch out now, one . . . two . . . three . . . Well, what are you waiting for?

— I don't dare.

— Pull! Pull!

The inspector pulled with all his might, and the chief began to howl and jump about in his seat.

— Curse your mother's religion! You onion head! Moses' arse! Spare tire! I told you to pull, not to break my finger!

— By Allah and the Prophet, did I break it?

— No, but just about. The chief wiggled his thumb, sucked on it, and stuck it under his right thigh to keep it warm. The inspector was very worried. He said:

— That's what got me into the police force. I can handle anyone with only

9

a handshake. That, soccer, and my Study Certificate made it possible for me to climb up through the ranks four at a time. Oh, when I think of how some of my colleagues are older than I, and still pounding the sidewalk, booted-up and helmeted in any kind of weather just to give a swift kick to the belly of those unlicensed vendors who don't bother to go to the market. Ah, by Allah and the Prophet, I'm lucky. I am privileged, as sure as two and six make . . . eight, that's it.

— Well, tie your cursed tongue in a double knot and safe-guard your place among the privileged, you crocodile head! Don't bother about roads and trails. Leave that to the Corps of Engineers, the "Cooperants" and the prisoner work gangs. Don't get mixed up in that. Stay out of politics, and get on calmly with your police work.

— You're right, chief. It's a worker's paradise being with you.

— You know you could be sacked from one day to the next because of a simple yes or no?

— Really? said the inspector.

— Oh yes, booted out like a bum. Put out without your pension. Without a pension! You who spend your time locking up dangerous "insectuals," do you know that you could find yourself behind bars one day?

— Like how?

— I'll tell you how. By wasting my time with your jabbering. We arrived here ages ago, and here you are still babbling inanities for over an hour. We haven't even gotten out of the car! What time is it? The inspector consulted his quartz watch, and pressed two buttons, one which said "Select month/date" and the other which gave the time.

— It's Friday, July 11, 1980. It is precisely noon, 13 minutes and 26 seconds."

— Mine says the same, said the chief holding out his wrist, but mine's better. It has an alarm. Well, let's not waste time. Tell me, was it some informant who gave you that classy gift?

— No! Not at all! I bought it with my own money. I certainly know that inflation gallops faster than a wild horse, and that the *dirham* is in a free-fall. But it was with the sweat of my brow that I was able to purchase this self-winding watch.

The chief waved his hands, as though telling him to be quiet. His wrist joint cracked with a dry snap.

— Ah, now it's loosening up, he remarked with a little satisfied laugh. When you shut up, and I can get out of this blasted car, I'll try to loosen up my arm and spine. I've got to stay in good shape to carry out these official missions with which my superiors thought fit to entrust me. For the past three quarters of an hour, I've been trying to show you the safe road, but you don't listen.

— I'm really listening, chief!

— No, you're not listening. You've been talking gibberish about roads and trails, and abusing the thumb of an officer. So open your ears and check out that flea market of a brain you've got. There's enough noise and worries in it, and not only the ones your good wife creates. Why bring bulldozers and politics into that marketplace of a skull? You were able to pay for that quartz watch on your wrist? That's fine, inspector. In fact, it's very fine! Tomorrow, in a year, or maybe two, you'll be able to buy a beautiful villa, like the big-shots, with maids and all that.

The inspector raised a finger to ask a question, or to say that it was his dearest wish, but the chief silenced him immediately.

— Shut your trap. Listen to this story and let's hope it will be a lesson to you. I'm going to tell you about my father. He was a cop, like me. He guarded French law, the commissioner's headquarters, and sometimes even his home. Most likely to keep the mosquitoes out. He didn't even pack a rod. All he had was a tiny club. In a word, he served the French establishment.

— Yet you, chief, you have a gun and serve our own regime.

— That's right, exclaimed the chief. You've finally understood! Carried away by his ardent patriotism, he had a very human face, quite sleek and round. His eyes were a beautiful black, shiny with joy.

— National Independence came, and the new generation, of which I'm a member, regained its dignity. My father was nothing but a watchman, a simple cop, with no power of decision, no responsiblilty. As for me, his son, I've got authority!! . . . maybe just a little bit, but that's enough for me. Authority. Never forget it.

— No, never, chief, I would never.

— There's a huge difference between our colonized forefathers and the free beings that we are. Authority. There's another difference. My father was at the bottom of the ladder his whole career while I'm a chief at age 35. I'm entrusted with arduous tasks. I undertake them on my own account and I have a sense of responsibility. I'm saying, and you listen well, that little by little, God willing, we are given more and more power. And if it comes to pass, I'll end up at the top of the ladder, so high up you won't even see me. You might hear my voice on the telephone, or on T.V. Believe me, there are some good things about the police force. It's a generous profession, as secure as the security of the State. You can make your own way, so long as you carry out government orders and leave the dishwater to the politicians.

Put in this confidential mood, the inspector immediately brought to mind patches of his childhood. He had tears in his eyes.

— My father, you know, had an oven. One of these public, neighborhood ovens where housewives would bring their round loaves of bread on a board to have them baked.

— Those were the good old days, said the chief. He sighed.

— Yes, like you say, chief, those were the good old days. My father wasn't the owner of the oven. He was only the . . . servant, yes, that's the word. He wasn't even paid. For baking six loaves, he was given a pierced bronze penny. He had a little dirt stall with nothing, not even a mat. Nothing but the oven in one corner, and heat in all weather. We were quite warm in winter. When my father opened the oven door, we'd have just enough light to see by. Otherwise, it was dark all the time. I can still see the staircase at one end of

11

the store, a straight ladder with rungs far apart. At the top of it, there was a little attic with two mattresses. That's where we lived. There were seven children, plus my mother and my father who baked the bread down below.

— So, what did you eat in those days?

— We ate bread. I got to tell you, chief, there were all kinds of bread, depending on how rich or poor the customers were. There was beautiful white wheat bread, as pale as the bourgeois types who stuffed it down their throats, as plump as their bellies or behinds; or barley or acorn starch bread, dry, thin and gray like the miserable people who were sustained by it. And then there were the intermediate breads, of the middle classes.

— It was the time of the French, said the chief drily.

— You're right, chief. It was their time. But I don't think I ever saw one of them come into my father's store. They bought their bread in the French bakeries.

— It was their colonialism, said the chief in a hard voice. It was their system of domination. You know that as well as I.

— Yes, you're right. It was all you could expect. So my father always managed to burn one or two of those chubby loaves. He'd get bawled out by the rich types, but he'd always swear by heaven or hell that there had been too much, or too little yeast. That's the way it was for us. We heartily ate that well-burned bread. That and the scraps my mother brought back to the house at the end of the day. She was a maid in a big house.

The chief yawned, then tapped his mouth shut. He said:

— Consider that today, there are no more loaves kneaded by housewives, burned or not. There's industrial bread that you buy in the supermarket wrapped in cellophane. There's even some which comes from "Djermany!" Can you believe it? That's really something!

— Sure, chief.

— Consider the magnificent evolution our country has seen in two generations, maybe three. Your father had nothing, and here you are, his son, assured of getting an official check every month, guaranteed by the government.

— Oh, I'm not complaining, chief, not in the least.

— You have a handsome uniform, and you can buy yourself a watch like an airplane pilot would have. You don't lack for anything. You are somebody. You have authority, and are delegated power. My, but the times have changed.

— I know, chief. My father died one day going down that old ladder. He broke his neck.

— Times have changed for you!

— Yes, chief.

— So stop going on about it. We've been here at our destination for a long time, and you keep bringing up the past. What good is that?

— No good, chief.

— Well then, shut up and roll down the window. Good God, it's stifling in here. There's no air.

12

It was a tinted window, like the windshield. The inspector had scarcely turned the handle twice when the chief began to howl.

— What the hell is that? What is this furnace?

— It's the outside air, chief. It's July and I'd been warned it hits hard. I've felt it before, in my father's oven.

— Roll up the window at once. At once.

The inspector rolled up the window and gazed at his chief. He took time to position his tongue, as though it were a quid of tobacco, before asking:

— What shall we do?

The chief stayed silent. He stared at his fingernails as though he'd find the answers there.

— You're the chief, chief. You have much more authority than I. What do you decide?

Beyond the windshield, spotted with the dried and mineralized remains of insects, was the aboriginal kingdom, eternity found again: the earth and the sun. There wasn't a shadow anywhere. The inspector didn't dare look too closely at the vein throbbing in the chief's neck. Timidly, he said:

— If I remember right, these mountain folk don't have bathrooms. They're hardly civilized. They don't even have water. Not a stream as far as you can see. Maybe a well? In that case, it must be very, very deep. At this time of day, it must be dry as a pebble. I've looked all around us, and I don't see anything. Two or three mud houses, some scrub brush, and up there, on the *djebel**, some *arganiers*, jujube and cedars. But that's really all, believe me, chief. This village seems empty, abandoned. Come on. Shall we go home? We have enough gas. Let's take advantage of it.

*Mountain

13

The chief turned completely towards him, his face contorted, and screamed at him:

— Damn your forefather's religion!

— I'm not a Jew, said the inspector, wiping bits of spittle from his face. I'm an Arab like you, chief, by Allah and the Prophet!

— You drone, you kettle head. Who stuck me with such an inspector? You can't anticipate anything . . . I should do everything by myself. You're incompetent. You should have informed yourself before leaving! There's always the weather service. You mongrel! I've really been had this time! You should set yourself up as a hairdresser, or a café waiter. You testicle-head!

— Yes, indeed, nodded the inspector, it's all my fault. Go on, get it all out of your system. That's what I'm here for.

— I'm going to brain you, said the chief, waving his fist at him.

— Better to beat up the sun. No doubt you could put it out.

— I'll can you!

— Right away? You mean I can get out of the car?

— Stay here! screamed the chief with all the lung power he was capable of.

Two or three minutes later, when he thought his superior had calmed down a bit, the inspector started up again, conversationally, as though nothing had happened.

— You can always say you looked all around, all over the place, from horizon to horizon, left, right, down below, up on the mountain and that . . . that you didn't find anything at all. I'll back you up, under oath. I'm ready to sign my name to it right away. This village isn't even on the map, even though it was the large scale map you and I looked at this morning. Just as well to say it doesn't exist. The best thing for us to do is turn the nose of this car right around and head west, or north, if you prefer, and spend our four or five day investigation peacefully in some hotel by the coast, with cocktails, a swimming pool, bathroom, a shower whenever we want, and lots of good food. We have an expense account, so money isn't the issue.

— Are you serious? asked the chief. His voice was low, his eyes fixed straight ahead.

— No, of course not. I was just joking to pass the time. There's no harm in that.

— Joke on your own time—silently!

— Sure chief. If I did it out loud, it was only to cheer you up. It's real hot in this car, and there isn't the slightest ventilation. Let's not talk anymore about this little beach-side holiday. It's fate.

— Shut up. You're keeping me from thinking.

— Right away, chief. I just thought of it: we're on a secret mission, right?

— Yes, why?

— As I was saying, we should stay unnoticed, incognito. So in that case, let me explain. I'm in civvies and you're in a chief's uniform. Any dolt would recognize it a mile away.

14

The chief glanced at his braided arm, lifted his booted feet and looked at them. And then he began to laugh.

— These peasants have probably never seen a uniform before in their lives. And in any case, I should wear it as proof of my authority. I've even thought that in case of difficulty, I should carry out my investigation in French. Yes, I'll pose as a Frenchman.

— With your dark brown face?

— What do you mean by that? Don't you know there are tanned Frenchmen?

— Yes, chief, there are some, I suppose. But I don't know what's the matter, maybe the rest of the chickpeas don't want to digest: do you suppose these mountain folk speak French, by any chance?

— We'll find out, said the chief. You're making me waste time. You talk on and on, and you haven't a single idea. Like they used to say, "Hello leads the conversation, and conversation leads the carrot." The decisions are mine to make, so here's what's up: there's a handle on that door. Lower it from the top to the bottom and the door will open. You get out, you open the trunk, and you take out my bags and my gun. Got it?

— Got it, chief.

— And lend me your sunglasses. I'll give them back to you at the end of the mission.

— With pleasure, chief.

2

The man was standing in the sun, hands clasped around a staff almost as tall as he. His chin rested on his hands. He was ageless—and, maybe, mindless. Immobile. In front of him, a spit-shot away, there was a red mule, equally immobile, eyes wide open, tail hanging down like a piece of unbraided hemp, and two skeletal sheep trying to graze on hay as dry as plywood. Aside from this faint evocation of grass, there was nothing—naked stone which squeezed in on the enclosure where the man and his beasts seemed petrified into eternity. No lizard, there was not even the breath of an insect. Below the path etched out by generations of peasants, there was the village, with its houses asleep and its little pebbled square. And above, like a mirage, there was the granite mountain crowned by cedars and jujube trees thirsting for water and life. Beyond the compound, within earshot, there stood a thorn bush thicket covered with age and dust. And on all sides, falling from the seventh heaven, the heat of the last judgment.

The man with the staff had heard the voice of rumbling steel rend the silence. A little later, he heard three knocks of metal against metal. Now he was hearing a pair of feet behind him scrambling over the rocks, moving along the path and invading his peace. He stayed still. He didn't turn around. Not a single fiber moved in that face, tanned by decades of sun, and burnished by the winds of all those winters. Two men were circling him slowly as though perhaps he were an apparition or a scarecrow. A voice in front of him said:

— We're hunters. It sure is hot. Doesn't this inferno bother you at all?

The peasant didn't bother to respond. It was pointless. He had two eyes, and they were good ones. One of these men carried a rifle over his shoulder, so he probably was indeed a hunter. The sun was somewhere in the sky, that was clear. As for himself, well, he wasn't particularly hot or cold. He was at peace with himself. His was not an impatient spirit. Besides, what good does it do to talk about it? That's why the face he presented to the man in uniform with the black sunglasses resembled that of an *ahuri*.*

— Is there any game around here? asked the chief.

— Some partridge? added the inspector.

The man moved his lips in silence, as though he needed to translate these words into a language known to him alone. He examined the faces of these two intruders, then their hands and feet. With a faint voice, he echoed:

— Partridge?

— Yes, partridge, said the chief. Are there any?

— Where? asked the peasant, after reflecting on the matter a bit. He rocked on one foot and then the other. The calluses on his feet were as thick as bicycle tires.

— Here, said the chief.

— Here?

— Yes, here.

The peasant snorted. Or maybe it was his way of laughing. His eyes were surrounded by an infinity of tiny wrinkles.

— There are some, he answered.

— Where?

— There.

— But where, there?

— Over there.

— Would you mind showing me? asked the chief on the verge of apoplexy. A vein as big as a telephone cable throbbed in his temple.

— You would like me to show you, son?

— Yes.

— Partridge?

— Yes, where are they?

— There, said the peasant.

Suddenly he threw his staff at the thornbushes and almost instantly a large bevy of partridge flew up, five or six of them, and they raced off low above the ground, in the direction of the mountain. In a moment they had disappeared behind the jujube trees. Then, the dust fell slowly to the earth, and silence reigned once again.

— That's quite clever, said the chief who was furiously playing with the bolt on his rifle.

— Yes, replied the peasant with satisfaction. They're clever, those little beasts, they scatter at the least sign of danger. Not pausing, he issued a brief, gutteral order to his hooved friend:

— Rrrrrra!

The red ass shook his ears and set off. Without hurrying, he trotted over in

*A devil or evil spirit.

18

the direction of the compound wall where there was a hole. He went through it and went into the grove, returning just as calmly with his master's staff between his teeth. The peasant took it, groped in the pocket of his long, earth-colored shirt, and offered a piece of sugar to the ass.

— Is that a mule or a dog? asked the inspector, his eyes popping.

The old man didn't answer. He had taken his staff back, clasped his hands over it, and rested his forehead once again. As if nothing had happened. As if words were devoid of meaning.

— Did you train him?

— He likes sugar, like all old people.

And that was it. The mule had returned to the same place, and was staring off blankly into space. Two sheep were standing by, one of them with a piece of thatch in his mouth which he wasn't even bothering to chew.

Time seemed to dissolve in the sun. Sweat flowed down the faces of the two men from the city: fatigue, as well as a kind of protest against destiny. The one in uniform was breathing from his mouth. He asked:

— What's the name of this village?

Words left his mouth like so many dry pebbles.

— The village? echoed the peasant in a thin voice.

— Yes, what's its name?

— The village.

— What's its name?

— Well, I don't know.

— It must have a name, insisted the inspector.

— Yes, "The Village." That's what we always called it.

— What do you mean, "we?" the chief exclaimed.

— The people of the village.

— Don't get upset, chief, the inspector interjected. Let me handle it. Leave your gun alone . . . Tell me, grandfather, where does the representative of the Central Power live?

— I don't understand, said the peasant after having thought about it a while.

— In every part of the Kingdom, there is The State, a representative of The State, said the inspector, enunciating his syllables as if he were addressing a simpleton.

The mountain man raised his chin, then his hand, as if to fend off the sound of words. These men from civilization had reached him, forcing him to become involved in their world, to think, respond, understand. He took his time gathering up his tranquility, sheltering it within himself as though to keep it hidden, then said:

— I don't know anyone by that name.

— What name? howled the chief.

— *Thustate*. And because he knew now that they needed lots of words before they could accept the evidence, he added with simplicity:

— I was born here, and I'm not particularly young. I don't know anyone in the area, man or woman, who carries that name: *Thustate*.

19

He waved his hand around the four points of the compass, outlining in the emptiness the parameters of the village; pointing out the earth and the sky, the living and the dead.

— No one, he concluded.

— At least there's a chief, a caïd?

— No, we are all poor here. We're all equal.

— How many people are in this village?

— That's hard to say, let's see ... There are some born, some dying ... 34, or 33 ... the people, I mean ... I'm not counting the donkey, or the two sheep here. The mule must be somewhere on the mountain.

— Are there many families?

— No, it's all one family. The Ait Yafelman family.

— But there must be someone in charge?

— We're all Ait Yafelman.

— So what is your name?

— Ait Yafelman, like everyone else. No difference.

— What is your first name?

— Oh, you mean the nickname my mother gave me when I was born ... That was a long time ago, a very long time ago.

— So what is it?

— Raho. I am the grandfather.

— So you're the chief?

— Oh, no! I watch the sheep. There are only these two left. A long time ago, there were at least 15 or 20. A real flock.

— Ah.

— Yes, that's life. And death.

— How about strangers? Are there any strangers in this village?

— Oh, no! We're all brothers. We all know each other. It's all the same family. The Ait Yafelman.

— I mean, except for the Ait Yafelman?

Raho scratched his head and looked at the mountain, and then at the plains below.

— People who aren't like us?

— Yes, said the chief. Strangers!

— There are some, concluded the old peasant. People who pass through and then leave. It's their destiny. There are some who come down from the mountain, and others who come up from the plains, like you and your friend. You can't stop the wind when it blows. And anyway, the village is open. There's no boundary.

— No stranger stops here, even for a day?

— Yes, some do. But those two stay with us for several days. They generally come at the beginning of spring.

— Ah? said the chief. (And the inspector repeated it like an echo: "Ah?")

— Yes, said Raho. Well-dressed people like you and your friend. They are never the same two, but they always resemble each other. They come with empty hands, rifle the houses and go through the caves on the mountain. When they leave, they take our animals with them. The last time, they took the goat. As a result, we have no more milk. There's nothing left but this donkey, these two sheep, and the mule. Like I told you. Each time, they say it's for the taxes.

The chief and the inspector looked at each other.

— I saw nothing about that in the file, did you?

— Not a thing, chief.

— The finance people should have given us their files immediately, without delay.

— Yes, chief. I'd say they are better equipped than we are.

— That file would have given us a solid foundation for our mission. Instead, I'm in danger of swimming in my sweat and nothingness!

— Yes, chief.

The peasant cleared his throat several times. He coughed timidly, and said:

— You could perhaps do something for us . . . perhaps you know these tax people. We have nothing more to give.

— They're strangers, said the chief bitterly. We're not even in the same agency. They keep everything to themselves.

— But maybe you know them? There's one in dark glasses, like yours—tell

21

them they better not come back or I'll call the wrath of God down upon your heads.

— Fine, fine, said the chief, trying to be conciliatory. I'll talk to the higher-ups, count on me. Good God, things can't go on like this. We'll find out who controls the country, the Revenue Service, or the Law. Hiding evidence in an investigation . . . impeding the wheels of justice! I'll take care of it right away, immediately!

— Right now? asked the inspector. We can go home, then?

— No, cried the chief. Afterwards! One thing at a time.

Raho heard and understood the basic meaning of the words. His worries were melting away: perhaps there was no basis for them. He had been right to listen and speak after all. He had been up for a whole day for the harvest promised to be a good one. Placing his hand on the helmet of the chief, he blessed him.

— In the name of the Most Merciful and Benificent God, may His peace fill your heart, and inspire your words and deeds forever.

— Good, said the chief, Good. Mmmmmm. I need to take a nap. I'm beat, grandfather. Tell me, where is your house? Where do you live?

— Not far from here.

— Where, which direction?

Raho glanced at him quickly, lifted his foot, and put it down exactly where it had been, where he was standing. Worry started to sweep over him again, confusing, piercing, the way he felt each time at the approach of danger—an army of grasshoppers still in the distance, or some other divine or human calamity. This son of Adam and Eve, however, had just promised him hope . . .

— Right here, he said. And sometimes over there, in the corner of the wall. When evening comes, I squat down, then night falls; then dawn comes.

— You sleep here in all weather?

— Yes.

— Even in winter when it rains?

— When it rains, it rains. Water from the sky is good for man and beast.

— And that doesn't bother you?

— Oh, I've got my hood, and I pull it down over my head. Sometimes I'm invited into one of the houses, but it makes me feel like I'm in prison.

— Where do the others live? Where are they?

— Who?

— The other members of the tribe?

— It's a family, not a tribe.

Suddenly, without warning, the chief flew into a rage. He bounded over to the peasant, his mouth set in a grimace, brandishing his rifle like a club, gripping its barrel with two hands. His voice was choked with anger, rising with his thwarted authority, then falling into the base pit of his primordial instincts. Civilization rises and falls, thus, like the gust of air from a bellows. And written constitutional law becomes what it once was, verbal and oral:

22

— You old, dry piece of shit . . . you're going to . . . I'm going to . . . I'll make you swallow the rest of your teeth, you dog of your father and your race!

The inspector had immediately intervened, taken away his gun, tried to calm him down, grabbed his sleeve and repeated with various modulations:

— Chief, chief . . . chief . . . chief!

He addressed him in French, thinking justifiably that this language had a good effect on him, which like a cool shower could wash off the slime of anger, and bring him back to reason and civilization:

— Chief, listen to me for a sec . . . this jerk . . . whatchya doing there, chief . . . Think a bit 'bout your official mission—take it easy . . . calm down!

The man of the mountain was as still as a rock. From his stomach to his eyes billowed waves of incomprehension. He took in the yells, the words, the hostility, the evil, and the distress also, but he couldn't put the meaning of it all together. Was it possible that a son of Adam and Eve could be capable of several tongues in his mouth, and be inhabited by so many demons? The man dressed like a city dweller or a tax collector was facing the one dressed like a hunter, holding his head with fear and courage, walking each step with him. Raho realized he was trying to calm his rage by murmuring sugary words and smiling like a fawning, abandoned dog. And maybe the barbarous dialect he was using was the devil's tongue . . .

— Chief, continued the inspector, don't put yourself in such a state! That guy's from the Middle Ages, you're from the double-ten century . . . Come on . . . .you're going to get yourself all upset with someone from the Middle Ages?

The chief inhaled and exhaled through his mouth. His fury started to subside. He said, in Voltaire's language:

— What are you saying? What are you jabbering about?

— I said, chief, calm down! I'm talking reason to you. He's a dolt from the Middle Ages. You're not going to chase away the dark ages, burn away the shadows! He's nothing but a savage, I tell you. He's got cat whiskers in his head. There's no brain in there. Nothing but a sponge.

— What a savage! cried the chief. You saw how he gave me a hard time! Whore of his race! Why did you keep me from impaling him?

— Fine, answered the inspector. Fine, you kill him, O.K. The gun goes "bang!" and the others take off. They're nomads. You think you'll ever get them back? And your official mission goes down the drain with them!

— Maybe you're right. You blab on and on, but you're probably right.

— I am right. Let me do it. You'll see. I'll talk to this Medieval artifact with medieval diplomacy. Stay put, chief.

The inspector turned to the peasant and said:

— Grandfather . . . Mr. Ait Yafelman . . . Raho, you undoubtedly understood what happened to my poor companion?

23

— No, said Raho, still standing immobile.

— He's tired, he has many cares. So the heat demon entered him, understand?

— Aha! You mean the *kouriyya*?

— Yes, exactly! The heat of the Sahara and the Sudan caused his blood to boil. The *kouriyya*, as they used to say. It suddenly swept over him and mixed up everything—cooked the works: his bowels, his brain, his spleen. A little more, and he'd have been back in the Middle Ages. But I cooled him down with certain, special words.

— Hey! What are you saying?

— Shut up, chief. In the name of a dead rat, let me do it. You'll mess up all my diplomatic efforts.

— It doesn't seem to me as though he's entirely regained his senses, said Raho slowly.

— It'll come, said the inspector, it'll come.

— There's still a little of the *kouriyya* in him. You see, son, over there under that pile of stones there's a root. If you chew it, it'll get rid of the *kouriyya*. It's the remedy. You want me to pull it up?

— No, no, said the inspector. He's cooling off.

He clasped his hands together and said seriously:

— Grandfather, we are God's guests.

Letting his staff fall, the man of the mountain came towards him, his eyes bright. All his wrinkles started to move, from the neck up to the base of his nose, and from his forehead down to his lips, like the silt of a delta, giving birth to a big, open smile. He hugged him, kissing him on the left shoulder, and said:

— Son, welcome to this village. And may your companion be welcome. Hospitality is sacred.

Around his neck, he had a string from which was suspended a bull's horn. He seized it with both hands, put it to his lips, and sounded two thin notes, followed by their echoes bouncing between land and sky.

— The Ait Yafelman are now notified. They are waiting for you up above. The donkey will carry you. He knows the path. Both of you can get up on his back.

— It will be too heavy a load for this little beast.

— Ha! said the mountain man. He does what he can, and does not do what he can't. Watch him at his task. *Aji*, come here, he called to his donkey. *Zid!*

With the single shudder of a nostril, one ear flat against his head, the other standing up like a post, the burro started to walk towards the chief, as though he had known in advance, from the beginning of animal eternity, that that one there was going to straddle him up by the neck, with the other behind him on the rump.

— He can, concluded Raho. Otherwise, he wouldn't have moved an inch. He helped them settle on, and put between them their two traveling bags, then said:

— Rrrrrra!

The donkey perked up the ear which had been horizontal, and moved philosophically ahead. Beyond the compound and the thornbushes, the police chief remarked:

— Bravo, inspector! You handled yourself well. We are where we're supposed to be. I'll make out a good report on you.

The inspector said nothing. He was thinking of his father, dead these many years—dead and buried, along with his epoch. When some traveler, stranger, or mendicant, poorer than he, would knock at the door of his little dark shop saying "I am God's guest," the oven's guardian smiled the same smile, full of joy, which the policeman had just seen on the face of this old man of the mountain. The path which led up towards the *djebel* seemed to lead down to the past. The air was dry. Their hearts as well.

Some twenty minutes, or twenty seasons later, Raho re-opened his eyes. He had taken off his *djellaba*, laid it out on the ground, and he had just completed his midday prayer with his eyes shut. That was religion, the five times daily tribute to Islam—just as he and the Ait Yafelman clan paid their tribute to the State, in the form of goats or sheep. And long before this State, there was another State which used to send a civil comptroller and a gendarme to the village just when they had had their worst harvests. The Mountains always stood, trees withered, and others replaced them. Life was always such. In Raho's secular memory, fed by generations upon generations, there was the memory of another earth, with verdant plains and hills planted with fruit-bearing trees. That's where the clan had lived. There was *grass*! The earth was generous, the fruits varied and numerous. How could a simple orange today compare? And then, like armies of grasshoppers, or others of

God's disasters, came the invasions of the men of God, of civilization, when men had swept the clan from where it had been to other horizons, far from the plain, farther still from the plateaus, always higher and higher, through the centuries of progress upon progress. Certain ancestors had converted to the religion of the occupiers, merely to gain peace, and to continue to live, even on higher and more arid ground. Others scattered and became nomads. And later, members of the Ait Yafelman clan had crossed the seas to participate in two world wars—and perhaps found peace there . . .

— The old ones of the village, and I, we will soon die, said Raho to himself. We've had our time. And our descendants? How high up will they have to climb? There's nothing left, up there on the mountain. Nothing but the frontier . . . They can't go down into the next country. And perhaps, who knows, peasants from the land of the Algerians are right now climbing in search of liberty and sustenance. But beyond that *djebel*, there's nothing more for us but the sky.

One after the other, he placed his hands on the ground, flat, the fingers spread. Well before civilization or Islam, beyond the events of History, there was the worship of the earth. From generation to generation, and from one flight to the next before the conquerors of every race, that old religion had perdured right up to him, by the oral route. Raho had done his duty, he had offered sincere hommage to the impersonal god of the monotheists. And now . . . with his hands, and through his pain, he was about to pierce the earth, to gulp down in himself the elemental and prodigious force of the earth. It was really simple: all he had to do was to spread himself out like the roots of a tree. The sap was there, coursing life, right down there.

Before him, the sun sparkled off the rifle of the *kouriyya*-maddened man, forgotten in the rush of his choler and madness and general unmanning that the mountain man had provoked in him. The clan had been warned, knowing now what it had to do . . . Above all, old Hajja . . . He had been right to blow his bull's horn twice: one note for hospitality for who cares what son of Eve or of Adam, even were he an enemy; and then, the second note, to apprise them all . . . In thinking of Hajja, a smile puckered his nose like that of a fox. Raho dropped to the earth, stretched out and kissed the earth. It was the voice of the nourishing mother who had told him to blow the horn two times.

3

Seated at the mouth of the cave, her legs stretched before her like a pair of hatchets, Hajja flattened with dry slaps of her palms balls of paste which smelled of rancid butter, and with one eye half closed and the other wide open in her olive-wood textured face, she contemplated the mule which was unloading its cargo of ill-tempered urbanites. Slowly, gently, taking the time to place the patty on a white hot stone between her legs, to turn it, to cook it, she finally opened her almost toothless mouth and said:

— *Marhba, marhba bikoum!* Welcome, welcome you two, sons of the plains, and the lower terrains!

But these words were preceeded by her laugh, as sharp and piercing as an orchestra of fifes and tambourines. The laughter in each of her words made them sparkle between the mountain and the sky, and it burst forth and burbled in a multitude of joys. When she was quiet, she slipped the patty over her shoulder. A hand reached out from the shadows and snatched it, while another held out another ball of paste. Hajja began to knead it, flattening it, taking her time, while a thin voice issued forth from the depths of the cavern:

— Thank you, Hajja. Oh, thank you. May God prolong your life!

Shuddering from his rump to his nose, the donkey raised his old head towards the sky and began to bray.

— You'll get yours too, Hajja said to him. Wait. Quiet your soul. Each one in turn.

— Is that an idiot or an idiotess, the police chief asked the inspector in rather coarse French. My *"pagole"* of honor, she can't be both at the same time, he added logically. It's not possible!

His knees bent, he gingerly massaged his kidneys with tender little strokes. His congested face was covered with a mixture of sweat and dust as well as all the toxic residues of anger; throughout this humiliating ordeal, his rear end had been battered and abused all the way up the trail by the dorsal spine of this wretched little Moroccan donkey who even now, that filthy beast, was laughing at him through his big yellow teeth. As for his uniform, that handsome symbol of authority made of guaranteed American wool, straight from the States like all police gear and their instruction manuals, well, it was stained, wrinkled, soaked in sour sweat, ripped by thorns and brambles, ruined! That was that! With no further delay, right there on the spot, he was going to lock up everyone, kill them all, birds in the sky included, no exceptions, by God! He blamed it all on his subordinate who stood there in the sun, mouth hanging open, arms dangling, watching Hajja wave a patty in salute, repeating in her laughter *"Marhba! Marhba!"* while from other caverns and holes in the mountains smug, gleeful troglyditic heads of different generations poked out, and ten, twelve or thirty throats sang out like a choir: *"Marhba, Marhba bikoum!"*

— What are they, crazies, madmen or idiots? howled the Chief of Police. Answer me now, before I turn you into chopped Christian meat!

— Oh, no, chief, jumped the inspector. It's not that at all.

— So what's this all about? Don't you see they're making fun of us? The inspector took a deep breath of hot air and said:

— Fear.

— What are you babbling about?

— It's fear, said the inspector.

— Who fears? Explain, be clearer, speak French.

— They're scared of you, chief, that's why they're laughing. The chief walked up to him, mouth open, his hands balled up into fists.

— So, you're giving me a hard time too?

The inspector stepped back and said:

— No, chief. That explanation didn't just pop into my head. I'll explain. You ever seen certain suspects that we bring in? They start giggling their heads off—before interrogation. I've seen loads of them. They laugh like hyenas, trying to ingratiate themselves. But they don't laugh later. It's the psychology of fear. It's simple, you see.

He swallowed his saliva and repeated:

— You see, chief?

— Aha. When you put it that way, I understand, said the chief with a strange smile. That's more reasonable.

— You're right, chief. And now, we've got to go through the motions.

— Through what?

— The motions. The formalities, customs. We got to respond to these tribal types in their own way.

— Aha, you're talking about their little ways and habits.

— That's right, chief, ways, customs, habits and banalities. You got to do the right thing, just like on the T.V. shows. Watch me, and do what I do.

He walked slowly towards Hajja, as though in a procession, hitching up his pants, smoothing out his jacket, straightening his sleeves. His face took on the forlorn expression of a lost child as he grew nearer to the old woman. He sat down cross-legged next to her, took her hands, kissing them several times while saying with great respect:

— Greetings to you, Mother. Bless me, little mother, and may the souls of your ancestors rest in peace, through the will of God and the Prophet.

The inspector found that these traditional tribal greetings floated back to him from his childhood, like flotsam on the rising tide. He had never seen his own mother by the light of day. When she returned home from her job as a domestic, it was always evening, and the little furnace-hole they lived in was always dim. Once he had been able to see her in the full light of a spring day, peaceful and contented, lying in the cemetery on a wooden bier which the grave diggers were about to lower into the ground. That was another time, before his soccer days and the police.

Now, here on the mountain, once more he smelled the familiar aged, clarified butter, the odor of pancakes without yeast which were turning golden and crispy on the hot stone, and especially the scent of cloves which rose from her hair and her patched, indigo clothes, preserving the body of this old peasant woman. She was of the same species as his mother: pure, simple, protected from the jackals of this world by her very inexperience, even by her lack of conscious thought. His mother had had no thoughts either, for that matter. With tears in his eyes, he turned to the woman and said:

— I am a *berrani*, one of life's orphans, a stranger to myself. Bless me, little mother, in the name of the Lord. Give me the sign.

With her forefinger, she traced on his forehead the ageless sign from time immemorial: a fish enclosed within a five-pointed star. Then, her hands folded on the head of the inspector, she said:

— Peace, peace, peace upon you! The peace of the mountain, and of the plain, of the desert and the trees, of the rivers and the sea. And what name has God given you?

— Ali. I am called Ali. I am a lost sheep, a stray.

At the touch of Hajja's hands, Ali relived the gray memories which for him represented the milestones and datelines of his life. He felt sobs rising in his throat, and he did not halt them.

— Peace, my son, said Hajja. You are from the city? From way out yonder?

— Yes, Hajja, Ali replied, hot tears coursing down his face. I am from down there, way down there.

— Hey, you, don't you think you're going a bit far? shouted the chief in 20th century French-speak.

— Is your friend thirsty? asked Hajja. Is that why his voice is so raspy?

— Yes, Hajja, he's thirsty. He is hot and tired and he's upset about the sun. He's not used to it.

— I'm going to get you for that, you crocodile head! Wait until you see the report I draw up on you: insulting a superior officer while carrying out his duty and doing it...doing it in the presence of strangers—suspects, no less!

— Oh! Hajja cried out, her voice full of sympathy. He sounds so hoarse, the poor man. His throat must be parched.

— Completely, agreed the inspector, wiping his eyes. Not to mention his spleen, intestines, bowels, heart and everything else. He's completely dried out, like that wonderful lamb meat that people used to dry with spices in the sun in the old days. Do you remember? It was before Independence and tinned goods.

— Oh, yes, I remember, replied Hajja, her eyes moist with the memory. I haven't eaten any in eight or ten years, maybe twenty. It smelled so good, and tasted of sunlight. It was delicious, so delicious! . . . Be quiet, child, she said in conclusion, quiet right now! You're making my mouth water. It's not nice to tempt an old bird like me with delicacies I can't even have.

— Yes, Hajja, I won't say any more. Curses upon my pig's tongue. I didn't say anything about that old meat. Nothing at all. Forget it. Forget it!

During all of this, the chief was falling apart, little by little, despite himself, overcome by a *force majeure*, abandoned by civilization's trappings, its taboos and interdictions, professional duty, and even the super-ego so dear to Freud; he was shaking, stomping his feet, and hammering the ground with his boots. Pebbles flew, and the dust swirled densely around him. In the meanwhile, the residents of the mountain crept out of their holes with rounded eyes and perked-up ears, like a rabbit at dawn; they collected in a horse-shoe curve about the chief: children, old ones, men and women, filled with intense, intense curiosity while the Chief of Police flailed his arms like an epileptic windmill and babbled in all the languages known to him: in his mother tongue, in French, in English, in poker-game American, beerhall German, in Wolof, in all the civilized languages in whose tongues he's ever been abused. He was like the Third World man who, aside from some cultural refuse, had absorbed from the West all the detritus of its values and gotten some armaments in the deal. He was evidently a long way from any form of ratiocination, and could do little more than low like a cow. It went something like this (although, mind you, I don't dare print it in its fullest flavor):

— Curses upon your pagan race! . . . I'm going to screw you, whore and daughter of a whore! . . . Oukc'est mon fusil que ch't'écrabouille les claouis à coups de crosse? . . . I'm going to blow your balls off you son of a bitch! . . . Bugger off! . . . Kleb des chiottes! . . . Schweinhalloufhund! . . . Banderkatolikouyyoun! . . .

— What's more, said Hajja, he's possessed. Poor fellow!

— He's doing a rain dance, said an old man. That's what he's doing. Get everyone out, even the children. Watch the sky!

— It seems to me, grandfather, that there hasn't been a drop of rain in a very long time, said a young man with glasses. (He was nicknamed the Sage, alias the Dictionary. He was constantly scratching his head.) Not since the time of the Franks, if my memory is correct.

— This isn't the time for a sermon, retorted a *sans-culotte* kid. We're not at the Mosque, so close your French Koran. Get the message, pea-brain?

— Give him something to drink, little mother, said the inspector, who was watching his chief's face turn the color of a beet. There must be at least a little water in this village, For pity's sake, we got to get his temperature down. He's making our government look ridiculous. It's the heat, the *kouriyya*.

— Some water! cried Hajja, turning around. Pass me the gourd. Quickly, quickly.

From the depths of the cavern rose the thin, reedy voice, dominating the blithering of individuals and the cacophony of nations, saying, word by single word, each one followed by a reflective pause:

— Fine, Hajja, here's the gourd. But-I-have-something-to-tell-you. Something-very-very-important.

— Pass me that gourd, replied Hajja, and shut your trap as firmly as you've shut your eyes for some time now. There is a son of Adam and the city who's about to breathe his final breath. His soul is being released through his eyes, his ears, and especially his mouth. I can hear the death-rattle.

— Fine, Hajja, here's the gourd. But-I-have-something-to-tell-you-which-can-brook-no-delay. It's-life-or-death.

The gourd passed from hand to hand in a succession of muted movements, while Hajja yelled into the cave, sputtering:

— I'd rather listen to a grasshopper than an ignoramus such as yourself. Or a fly, or even a wasp which the Lord created to harrass human beings. So be quiet! I'll listen to you in a bit.

— Fine, Hajja, but-what-does-that-mean, in-a-bit? Suddenly turning around, Hajja tossed a patty at him and said:

— Catch it, eat it, and shut up!

— Thank you, Hajja . . . may-Allah . . .

— In a bit means in a bit. The sun is still high in the sky, night has not yet fallen. Are you Beelzebub's whelp or a grandson of mine, as I used to believe?

— Allah forbid! replied the thin voice hurriedly. I have nothing to do with Hell's demons. I am your grandson, as well you know. Basfao is my name.

— Well, Basfao, stop irritating me with your silly remarks. I'll hear you out in a bit, in other words, before the end of the day. And that's an infinity of time. And I'm sure that whatever you have to say will be little more than the braying of a donkey, as usual.

— Oh, no, Hajja, responded the voice, which little by little had regained its tempo and composure. Not this time. We-have-nothing-to-eat. Except-some-patties-and-a-few-beans. So-Basfao-asks-you-: What-do-we-have-to-offer-our-guests?

— Be quiet, said Hajja, with some asperity. Lower your impertinent voice.

— Fine, Hajja, I-will-lower-it. But-these-people-have-requested-the-hospitality-of-Allah-and it's going to be *l'achoum*, a shameful disgrace, an empty-pot, or-close-to-it, with-five-or-six-beans-for-each-one! Haha!

— Lower your voice more, pull in that corrugated tongue of yours and suck it down to your belly! I know perfectly well there's nothing in the cupboard. So why bother to remind me of it?

— Grand-mother, Hajja, maybe-this-man-is-going-to-really-die? That-would-at-least-take-care-of-half-this-debacle-haha!

— Quiet. No, he is reviving, thank Allah. He's just had some water and his friend is patting his back and speaking to him that devilish tongue, probably to exorcise the demons from him. He's a fine man. Moreover, his name is Ali, like one of the Caliphs in the olden days. You remember those legends which I used to tell the family, during the time when there were such things as blessings, grass, and the flock. There was milk and cheese in abundance, dates, and . . . and sun-dried meat!

— There's-nothing-here-but-a-few-beans-and-bare-footed-farmers-haha! And-the-Caliphs-of-Petrol! But-talk-on, Hajja, tell-me-what-you-see.

— It's not easy. There is too much dust, too many cries, too many voices. You hear them, Basfao?

— Yes, it-echoes-like-a-tempest-in-the-cavern, but-I-understand-none-of-it. Help-me-out, Hajja, tell-me-what-they're-doing.

— Well, they're continuing to cool down that man. Five or six Ait Yafel-man are sprinkling him with water. The gourd is now empty, but the man has been saved, he's shaking himself off, his face is less red, thanks to Allah.

— So-he's-back-again, fine-and-famished. Let's-prepare-for-the-swarm-of-locusts!

— Quiet! Please shut up! You're keeping me from seeing what's going on; your asinine words cloud my vision.

— Fine, Hajja, I-won't-say-anything-more.

For some time, the sounds of the twentieth century dominated the mountain. Nothing else. And then Hajja turned to the cavern and said:

— We could perhaps sacrifice one of the two old sheep which we still have left?

— Those old carcasses? retorted the blind man at top speed. Raho says they're nothing but skin and bones. Besides, what are the rest of us going to eat this winter? Have you thought about that? Our two guests will live . . . and the Ait Yafelman will die.

— Oh, shut up.

Suddenly, she burst out laughing, the fifes and tambourines of her joy leaping to the four points of the compass. She cupped her hands and shouted out:

— Bourgine! Hey Bourgine! Where on earth are you? Bourgin-e!

— Here, Hajja, a serious voice responded to her trumpeting. I am here.

— You still have your card game going?

— As always, Hajja, and how! Mountain poker.

— Well, tether the mule and come see me. Come take charge.

34

— Alright, Hajja, alright! said Bourgine, with a loud laugh. I'll be right there.

— Now-I've-got-it, said the man in the cavern. You're-still-a-quick-thinker-Hajja. You-haven't-grown-old.

— Then for the love of God, stay quiet. If not, I'll pry your mouth open and paint your tongue with tar. Make things ready for our guests, over there, where it's cool. They're going to want to relax, take off their traveling clothes. They're full of dust, fatigue, and age. I will brush them and hang them in the sun while they take their nap. We must take care of these men from the plain down below.

— I-understand, repeated the blind one with a snort and a whinney.

— Fine, so go out and air yourself. You're going to get all moldy in there. Air out your head!

— O.K., Hajja. I'm-going-right-now. At-last-I-will-be-able-to-take-part-in-the-festivities.

The blinding whiteness of the sun was followed by the cool obscurity of the cavern which had been carved into the side of the mountain by generations of men intent on resisting the tide of human events. The interior walls were damp and soothing, the earthen floor was scattered with old worn pelts. The chief of police, bundled up in a stiff, rough *djellaba*, raised himself up on his elbow and studied the inspector, who was sleeping seated with his mouth hanging open. He was full of sadness and there was a touch of bitterness as well; he felt depleted in the face of these animal instincts. There was no other word for it: animal! It was extraordinary! There was a man whose parents and forefathers had been colonized, dominated, crushed . . . and yet, by the grace of free, sovereign and democratic government, this man had become his, the chief's, own second deputy in command. He had a little package of authority, he had dignity and the respect of his fellow citizens. He could command, direct and carry out! And what whas he doing here? He was sleeping like the rest of the Third World! You didn't have to look very far for an explanation. The answer was clear and self-evident: those who ran the superpowers are in a state of constant vigilance. They don't fool around! They're not at all like this silly inspector with his oversized gums who, left alone, flees duty and loses himself in a secular and fatalistic sleep. What's more, scattered around him on a sheep's skin he's left all the various totems of his authority: a pair of hand cuffs, his notebook and pen, his official police identity card and badge, and his folder of papers! Giscard d'Estaing, Brejnev, Carter, Mrs. Thatcher, they weren't off sleeping in some grotto like a bunch of animals!

Collecting all his planetary energy, flexing the muscles in his neck, the chief bellowed out in a thunderous voice:

— Wake up!

The inspector yelped as he turned a somersault.

— Wake up! You've been snoring ever since we left the capital. I've got to do everything around this miserable place. You're useless to me. You are a worthless object. That's what you are. Inert and useless.

— I wasn't sleeping, chief, by God and the Prophet

— Oh, you were thinking again? Is that it?

— Oh, no, chief, not that. Never again. You're the chief, so you must do the thinking, not me. Not me, he repeated shaking his head back and forth.

Trying to stifle a long yawn, he looked like a boa swallowing a chicken, and added:

— I was relaxing, taking a break.

He finished his yawn, smiled from cheek to cheek, and explained himself in precise, mathematical terms:

— I wasn't sleeping, I was relaxing. There's clearly a big difference.

His eyes were expressionless and his face innocent.

The chief shook his sausage-like finger at him and said, even more menacingly:

— Well, we're going to find out right now if I'm an imbecile or a police chief to whom one owes respect and consideration. Listen up.

To the inspector's way of thinking, the first of these two hypotheses seemed the more suitable, but he didn't let it show. He banished this revolutionary thought much in the same way the pilgrims to Mecca stone Satan. Which is why he buckled on his helmet before attending to the chief's next words.

— Listen to me closely: What were you taking a break from? Why were you relaxing?

— It's simple, chief. Very clear.

— What's so simple, you simpleton?

— Well, the inspector replied slowly, I was awaiting your decision, chief. Your orders. I think it's quite clear, as surely as three and three make six in French. It should be even more obvious to you. I was relaxing while awaiting your instructions.

He yawned again, and said:

— There, you have it.

— Hmmm, said the chief. Hmmmmm!

— Yes, that's right, replied his subordinate encouragingly. These things are all quite simple. There's no need to meditate on them. It's enough to sit back and relax a bit.

The chief scratched his head, then, very deliberately, his ear lobe and his nose. He said:

— It smells like a billy goat.

— Me! demanded the inspector somewhat fearfully. What I just said, or me, personally? (He immediately started to sniff his *djellaba*. It had holes in it and had been repatched often. It was the color of sand, and if it smelled of anything, it smelled of time immemorial, with perhaps a whiff of old mutton—but certainly not like a billy goat, no indeed.)

— Not you, said the chief, in here, in this cave. Don't you think so?

— What? Oh yes, certainly, in my humble opinion... I really do think, of course...

— Of course. So what's your opinion? Let fly your noble thoughts!

— Well, it's my opinion that it smells rather more like poverty.

— Oh, really, said the chief, straightening up in his seat.

— Yes, chief, it smells of poverty, and of ignorance. It's an odor I know well. You don't need to be a policeman to recognize it.

— Explain.

— Sure, chief, it's like an ox.

— What do you mean, an ox? What are you trying to express?

— An ox, chief, is not particularly intelligent. As the name would indicate, an ox is a grazer and its thoughts are fueled by hay.

— So? I don't understand.

— Nevertheless, it's evident: the ox pulls the cart, and the peasant follows the cart. You put ignorance in place of the ox and what do you find following? Misery and poverty. See, it's quite simple.

For a long moment, the chief studied his fingernails as though he were questioning them, moved his toes, and considered them as well.

— Free up your mind, he said, and I will give you some paternal advice.

— Yes, chief.

— If you like, say that this grotto is poor, sordid, medieval, just right for sheltering this handful of primitive mountain people. But don't talk to me about oxen or the philosophy of history.

— O.K., chief. May God help me.

— You see, son, you're a good fellow, but very, very complicated. You try to reason things out like a chief, and that's what spoils your character. That mixes up your thoughts with your words. It's up to me to reflect on things. You only have to carry them out. I've said it over and over again to you.

— Fine, chief, think a bit and tell me what I should carry out. What are your orders?

— See here, exclaimed the chief. Would you like me to rush headlong into things, like an unthinking fool? You should learn that real thought is something very important. It's not to be improvised!

— Yes, chief.

— Take out your notebook and write down what I'm going to tell you.

He waited patiently while the inspector readied himself to receive his wisdom, then began to dictate:

— Write: "Today, 11 July, 1980, the chief said, quote: True and authentic thought is like a seed; it is sown in the fertile soil of the brain—dash—and evidently, fertile brains are rare. For germination to take place, you need cultivation, ad hoc, intellectual fertilizers which not everyone possesses, alas . . ."

— Should I write, "alas?"

— If you wish, write down everything. It's important for your future. I was saying then, ". . . intellectual fertilizers, a certain adroitness, attention to all

37

the details, irrigated by morality, as plants need to be watered." You follow me? It isn't too arduous for you?

— I follow you, chief. It's a pleasure to listen to you. So, therefore, thought comes from the brain in springtime and results in a flower, or a cactus, or maybe even a tree. Is that it?

— Close your notebook, and stash your pen somewhere, said the chief sorrowfully.

— Fine, chief, right away. It's practically impossible to write in this gloom.

— Especially with the dimness of you mind. As you were noting earlier how the ox pulls the cart—I, I drag you along like a ball and chain.

— That's it, chief, you're my ox. What would I be without you? So, what do I do? What orders should I execute? We better start thinking of our official mission. Time flies.

The chief stretched himself out comfortably on his couch, gathered together a bundle of old clothes and stuffed them under his head for a pillow.

— I'm going to think things over, carefully, while I take a nap. The cerebral activities of my brain can proceed by themselves, and you don't need to be part of the process. Don't disturb me in my deliberations.

— It wouldn't occur to me, believe me, protested the inspector. So can I go back to sleep?

— If you like, but don't snore. I don't want you disturbing my thoughts. And be ready to get up in an instant. Don't wake me, however, unless its a matter of some highly official communication.

— Fine, chief, replied the inspector in a mumble.

— What I would like to know is this: Are you with me? I mean, for order, discipline and duty? Or are you perhaps on the side of these scabrous peasants . . .

— Me . . . me?

— . . . as your earlier attitude might lead me to suppose? For heaven's sake, let me finish! I can understand that your humble origins, your very, very humble background might incline you towards them, but I really want to know. So tell me. Articulate, express yourself clearly. I can't stand it when you mumble. One of these days you'll be hung up on all that rusty wire inside your head, and I won't be around to get you out of it, even with a bulldozer. Don't count on me.

— It's simple, chief, "All for one, and one for oneself."

— What's this gibberish? What are you talking about, "Awful one and one four one"?

— It's what the Americans say; "Pure newwoolmark extra guarantee." It's the same thing, chief.

— Are you trying to keep me from sleeping?

— Oh, no, chief, don't think such a thing. You asked me a question and I am answering clearly. You and I, we're together for good, like the French and Americans say. All for one and one for oneself. It's easy, it's very simple.

38

— Be quiet, *taiseux*! yelled the chief in French. Let me sleep.

— O.K., chief.

An instant later, as though by enchantment, there was nothing but two open-mouthed, snoring policemen, all civilization suspended by their sleep. The official mission could wait.

● ● ●

Seated at the entrance of the grotto like a she-bear, Hajja sighed and said quietly:

— They are finally asleep, these two children of the plains. Overcome by their own words.

— Do I still get a commission? asked Bourguine.

— Now more than ever, she replied. But lower your voice. With these children from out there, you never know. The lightest noise could waken the warriors within them. Whisper!

— I am yours to command, Hajja, murmured Bourguine. Standing in the sun with shaven head and bare feet planted on mother earth, covered with a peasant's robe tied with a rope, he was rapidly flipping a deck of cards from one hand to the other like an accordian, a spiral, a spray of water, catching them on the back of one hand.

— So what shall I take, Hajja, tell me!

— Some meat, she said right away, without the least hesitation. Some meat for all of us and our guests. And some couscous for hospitality's sake. It's been a long time since we tweaked the devil's tail. But Bourguine, you're sure you can do it? You'll succeed? Really?

— You mind your business, Hajja. This is my job. The cards know me. See the way they move? Would you like a donkey? Here you go!

— Lower your voice and stop laughing. May Allah's blessing go with you. Add a little butter, a pound. A good pound, OK?

— Let's get two, added Bourguine. You'll have some nice, yellow butter.

— Ah, that's my favorite! May Allah grant you long life, my son. How about a little honey, just a little pot of it. It's good for an old woman with a sweet tooth. It's nourishing, and helps the circulation.

— Fine, said Bourguine, flipping the cards over his shoulder and catching them behind his back. I've got it all down in my head: a whole sheep with all four legs, a sack of couscous, a couple of pounds of butter, and a jar of nice, rich honey.

— Shhh, son. You're making my mouth water.

— How about some vegetables? Would you like some?

— Oh, yes, I forgot about the vegetables, they're essential. Some squash, chick peas, fresh peppers, and some hot chili peppers, not too many. Bring also some spices so the meal will be delectable and linger long on the tongue. Some "top of the shop" especially. It's particularly good for simmering with the stew. Some onions and garlic, also. Can you really get all that?

— Easily. Don't you worry.

— That's wonderful. When I go to Mecca, if I'm lucky, before I die, I'll say a special prayer for you. Oh, add some raisins.

— A bag of raisins, repeated Bourguine, as he magically made his cards disappear under his robe. And some bread? You forgot the bread. Would you like some milk? Just say the word, and it's yours. And not to worry. Today, we've got it all.

— May Allah protect you and watch over you, little one. Do you think . . . do you think we could . . .

— Yes, what is it? You can have whatever you want. All that we need to start with is a little capital. Nothing happens without capital. There's some philosopher up in the northlands who used to say that. I think his name was Kalamass.* Don't hold back, Hajja. Your wish is my command. It will be a gift for you.

— . . . Perhaps, some chocolate. Just one bar. It will last the rest of my life. Oh, I'm a glutton, aren't I?

— Ten bars, rather, let's say twenty. Chocolate's not very heavy.

— May these mountain cedars, and the palms of the desert impart their strength and vigor to you. Are you going to be able to carry all this on mule-back? . . . Where is the beast, I don't see him. Didn't you tie him up?

— No need for a mule, Hajja. Those two fellows in there have a car. Ha! It's sitting there doing nothing in the village square.

— Lower your voice and stop gloating. And how are you going to get it started? It's not a donkey. You can't kick it and say to it: "Rrrrrra! Hua!" It's made of iron and you need a key.

— I don't need a key, Hajja.. With this piece of wire, I could get a jet plane going and head for the seventh heaven.

— But won't its iron voice rumble and wake up its masters?

— No way. Nothing like that at all. The mountain is high, and the plain is low. This car will make it down without motor, without noise. It will roll free. As for the return, you say? Sure, it's a steep path, but I've thought it out: the mule will be there, with a big, strong rope to pull it. That mule is solid, he is.

— Fine. You have my blessing. So who are you going to play cards with . . . and maybe beat?

— I will surely win, don't worry about that. The cards slide between my hands like soap. You remember Saïd, Hajja? The guy who owned one of the houses in the village? He's now called Moul Bousta, Mister Post Office. He's head of the postal service, somewhere down there in the high plains. Five or six years ago, he was just a peasant like us. Now he's rich and pretends not to know anyone. But he sure likes poker. Ah, little mother, am I going to clip him, ha ha!

— Don't laugh. It's not very nice what you're going to do.

*Karl Marx

40

— Oh, really? How much did you swipe out of his wallet?

— I don't know, Bourguine. I don't know how to read. It was a very pretty bank note, and it seemed to tell the legend of King Solomon. Try to bring that one back, or something like it.

— No problem. There will be little ones, big ones, and great big fat bank notes. "Kalamass" was right when he said, in life you've got to have capital. The Russians were peasants like us, slaves. And now they've got push-button atomic. *Baraka*!

— May Allah go with you. But bring back that bank note, or something like it, so I can put it back in the wallett. Then nobody will find out about it. After all, we're people of good will and honor. I wouldn't want anyone to think we are thieves. That wouldn't be right.

— Who would ever say such a thing? You just took a little loan which you will reimburse this very evening, with some interest even: a dinner the likes of which we haven't seen in years. Just think of it, Hajja. Think of the honey and chocolate!

With that, Bourguine walked off into the sun, shuffling his cards back and forth like a rainbow.

Seated in the middle of the enclosure on a flat stone, between the two parched sheep and the motionless donkey, Raho gazed at the setting sun. Everything devolved from it, all was encompassed by it. It was the sun which made plants germinate, and which withered them, and made them die. When a man had spent almost all of his existence between the earth and the sun, he could do no other than to accept life. The earth was denuded, without water, barren for generations. Sun was sovereign. Why struggle, initiate anything, construct a shelter— protect oneself? Against what? Heat is the force, the stripping away, a gift. So many things in this world are useless, so many that man has laboriously erected, buying shadows at the expense of light. This Islam, this religion which somehow touched him, Raho, wasn't it born way back in time, way back in the arid desert, between the sand and the sun— nothing else? Like Islam, and his own destiny, one was born from the belly of one's mother, naked, and one returned equally so into the entrails of the nourishing mother earth. Your skin and flesh were witness to this truth!

The rays of the sun baking on the horizon transformed the face of the old man into shades of copper and pewter; then they reached his arms, his legs, his entire body as he undressed and threw off into the distance those articles which, throughout the day, had hid him both from others and from himself. Squatting down, he stretched his arms forth, and drew them slowly back, as though gathering in an armful of golden, ripe wheat, and he began to wash himself with the light of the setting sun.

All religions, whether from the Orient or the Occident, or elsewhere, had only inflicted thought upon him. Yet he, Raho, had been born without thought and would die so. It was so easy to live. Slowly, he bathed his face in the sun's ruby rays, and washed his hands three times. And then he prostrated himself before this dying star.

41

This life's journey which was almost at a close, what had it really been? For other men who lived on other mountains, near and far, on the plains, on earth or on water, it had been what it could be. Raho himself had no notion, no consciousness of what his life had meant. It had been that minimal. Other men had their own destinies. As for Raho, he had completed his journey. One more offering owed the sun.

For the village, the community, almost half of whom were his descendants, this life's day had seen the intrusion of two strangers left to themselves. They were as aggressive and unhappy as the conquerors of any race or religion who had ever unfurled their banner in the pages of history. Had any of them managed, for all that, to conquer the sun? Suddenly, the face of the man of the mountain dissolved into an ocean of wrinkles which slowly flowed to the corners of his mouth—and Raho, like a wolf, started to laugh noiselessly at the mere memory of the legendary Commander Filagare.

4

— Yes, said Hajja, Commander Filagare was a peasant like us, yes, yes indeed.

And then, she burst out laughing. And all the members of her family, near and far, made the mountain ring with their laughter.

Everyone rejoiced at the prospect of the sizzling feast, and all were gathered round, sitting on their haunches, all, that is, except for the chief, who was perched on a packing crate, thinking, no doubt, to preside over the meal, and Hajja, whose legs stuck out straight in front of her in their customary position. The Ait Yafelman stuck their hands deep into the platter and extracted generous portions of food, saying, with their voices charged with emotion and gratitude: "Praise the Lord!" while forming balls of couscous and vegetables ranging in size from a pigeon egg to a melon, depending on the age or the hunger of the consumer. The meat, a delectable treat the taste of which they barely remembered, they dubbed, "the victim" or "Ould Brahim" (son of Abraham). An eager hand would reach into the depths of the platter, tear off a chunk, and offer it to one's brother seated next to or across from one: and like that game of tug of war which one played as a child (and which is still played in Western schools to develop the biceps and will power, during gymnastic training), each one would pull as strongly as possible towards oneself, and before one knew it there would be two pieces of meat from one, without the benefit of fork or knife. There were five or six courses, presented on carefully carved platters, each having been prepared in one of the family caves and brought up onto the mountain heights, where the cedars and jujubes stood tall like silent sentinels. Around each platter, there were five to seven guests. And, here and there, pine torches illuminated the scene like lit Christmas trees. Those who were in the shadows didn't much care: they knew well the path to their mouths. In any case, it was one feast, one family. Whether in shadow or light, there were no sociological or political distinctions among them.

From everywhere, numerous voices spoke almost simultaneously, a constant chain of sound:

— Thank you, Hajja, thank you for this sultan's feast!

— Oh, Hajja, said Bourguine, while digging into the platter with a wide-open hand, I replaced the paper which showed the legends of Solomon back into the leather case. And as you know, the mule was indeed able to haul that iron machine back up here. She took her fuel from the wind and the sky, I swear it.

— All of a sudden we've been blessed with God's grace, don't you think? interjected a woman who was perched high up. Life is good. Yesterday, it was a big zero.

— "It was a long time" said the bespectacled young man who was nicknamed "the Sage" alias "the Dictionary." His accent was purest Oxford and the words fell from his mouth like so many fragments of food—something like: "It weuz eu lonnn teuim!"

— He's speaking English, chief, said the inspector with his mouth full. He swallowed violently and added: Is he a suspect?

— More likely, he seems to be one of these "insectuals."

— Oh, Hajja, should we keep some of this food for tomorrow, for winter, or should we accept it as God's gift?

— Chew! begged one mother. You're going to choke on your food. Chew! You've got plenty of time. The food isn't going to run away.

— It's what I've always said: If Hajja has anything to do with the cooking, you can be sure it'll taste like one of those delights of paradise which the Koran promises us.

— May you live long, Hajja, you are our sustenance.

— Hajja, oh Hajja, repeated Basfao like an echo. I have something very important to tell you.

Seated at the center of the voices, Hajja heard them all, as though she had a dozen pairs of ears registering each word, listening even to those who were not members of the family and who were therefore reluctant to participate. Calmly, but in different tones, she began to respond in order of priority—first, to Basfao, then to the man who worried about tomorrow, then to the Sage:

— Eat and be in peace! There is nothing more important at this time than to be at peace with your stomach!

— And you, over there, try to make up for lost time, if you like, but don't gorge yourself silly. Relax!

— As for you, you peasant with glasses, one of these days, your tongue is going to turn backwards in your mouth. You shouldn't make fun of the words Allah gave us.

— But what did I say? protested the Sage. I said, "it's been a long time since . . ."

— You were twisting words, she interrupted.

— It was English. I learned some when I was a porter at the hotel in the capital, for heaven's sake. I had to understand what the millionaires were saying to me when they tossed me a tip! "Hey, boy!" they'd say, "Taxi! Get a move on!" And when the taxi would come careening, they would say: "It was a long time!" In other words, in our language, *It's been a long time since we've cracked a tile.* Even if they gave the cabbie a destination, he obviously wouldn't understand. "To the airport!" they'd yell. And of course I had to translate. I'd tell the driver, "They want to have a bite down at the port. Don't you have a cousin who has some joint in the *medina*? So take off, and don't forget my commission." I got fired from the hotel, and I sure don't know why. Maybe because I played favorites with the guys from the *medina*. You think that's possible?

But Hajja was no longer listening to him. It was this way: the people from the plains, and even he, had twisted the language just as they had ruined the countryside. They needed two round pieces of glass just to recognize their own people! And a watch around their wrist to figure out what was obvious to any peasant: the position of the sun in the sky. Well, he hadn't been back home for all that long. And the mountain had the patience of rock . . .

Furrowing into a plate of food, Hajja extracted the choicest morsels—sheep testicles—and presented them to her two special guests, her hands extended toward them, a gland in each hand:

— Please, take them, my sons, eat, eat! You are at home here. The best pieces are for you two.

Inspector Ali took the proffered testicle without the least hesitation.

— By Allah, he cried, beaming. That's just what I love. Providence was good to bring me here.

And he began to chew, the hormonal juices dribbling out the corner of his mouth which he slurped back up with his pink, agile tongue: what nectar! His eyes were bright. Watching him eat like a retarded person, governed purely by instinct, the chief of police could not help expanding his concept of what the Third World was all about. The Shah of Iran had been forced to flee by the forces of ignorance and because those savage Persians were incapable of comprehending the evolutionary measures which the Shah advocated. Who could doubt it? The State television and the government press had both announced this quite clearly. And the State certainly couldn't make mistakes in such matters! Sadly eying this soft, dripping thing which he held between his thumb and forefinger, like a tiny drowned rat, he rapidly thought of all the good things in life—and life meant maturity, responsibility, progress. And what did he, the chief, eat in the old days? Soup and couscous. And look at what he had to put up with here. And now that he had evolved into a chief worthy of his name, he consumed civilized, evolved food at the police cafeteria: wonderful fried foods, tinned goods from highly industrialized countries, nice white bread. In the restaurants of the European quarter of the city where he often had lunch with other chiefs, he, unlike many of his fellow citizens, felt like he was right in the 20th century: a tablecloth on the table, clean bright silverware, a waiter dressed like a field marshall, a frosty glass of whiskey and a cigar with a classy label which he puffed away at just like Churchill. It was quite simple: the clientele was likewise distinguished, elite, including powerful tourists who settled their bills without seeming to pay, with nothing, that is, but a credit card. He also would carelessly offer one of those cards: American Express, Visa, Interbank . . .

Thank you, sir, the waiter would answer politely, Merci, monsieur. Danke schön . . . in all the languages of the hard currencies.

— I can eat it if you're not hungry anymore, said the inspector.

— No, no, interrupted Hajja. You've had your share, you're too greedy. Don't be so selfish. It's for your colleague, don't you see?

She turned toward the aforementioned colleague.

— Don't be talked out of it, my son. It's the one remaining testicle. Eat it while it's hot. It's yours. Would you like some cumin on it?

With a wave of disgust, followed immediately by a wave of professional conscientiousness, the chief of police started to gnaw on the morsel of tepid sexuality. He reflected on his official mission. He had to see it through, and in order to do this, had better conceal his real feelings, his personal, intimate universe. Wasn't he already in place, clothed in a filthy *djellaba* like one of these backward aborigines, with an old bag for a napkin on his knees? Duty before all else. The State.

— Yes, said Hajja, as though these verbal preliminaries were but appetizers for her principal discourse, Commander Filagare was a peasant like us. He was nothing but a man from the mountain. I believe that he was already old. Nothing had ever happened to him before that day.

— What day, Hajja? numerous voices asked. Tell us the story!

She dismissed these importunate words with a wave of her hands as though they were so many mosquitoes buzzing in the night.

— No, no! she cried out vehemently. This story is not for you. You've heard it thousands of times. Stop clamoring, you're keeping our guests from listening.

— What day was that? asked the inspector, wadding up a good-sized ball of couscous.

— What Commander? added the police chief. He was attempting to chew the remains of the sheep and his face was set in a grimace.

— Ha, ha! laughed Hajja. He had never been a commander before, he was just a peasant like us. He had no history, none behind him, and none to look forward to. Neither past nor future. He was happy and at peace with himself. Would you like a hot pepper?

— What? replied the chief, surprised at this unexpected question.

— It calms the stomach, answered Hajja. (She gazed at him from the depths of her eyes). It helps excavate your insides, clears a path in your stomach so there's room for the rest of the meal.

— No, no thank you, said the inspector.

— No, not you, she retorted. You didn't have any problem eating. And so, one day, he went down into the neighboring country, two chickens tied foot to foot, and a basket of eggs in his arm.

— Which country? asked the chief.

— Down there, on the other side of the mountain.

46

— Algeria?

— That's it, the land of the Algerians. That's what it's called, but it's not right. They're just Berbers like us, our brothers.

— Ah? said the chief. Fine.

— Wouldn't you say so? It was a spring day, and he went to the market of a small city in the land of the Algerians. Oh, it wasn't far, a half-day's journey. There were eggs in those days, and even hens. And so the old man went to sell them to those who didn't have any, and bring home what his own family didn't have: flour or tea, for example. The Algerians and the Berbers around here do each other favors.

— Ah, ah, said the chief.

— Yes. That day, he did not know what was awaiting him. He left in the morning at dawn and was to have returned in the evening, simply one day's time. What is your name, my son?

— Me? said the chief. Oh, I'm a city man.

— This old peasant didn't know that Allah was angry on the other side of the mountain, in the land of the Algerians. There was war. What name did Allah give you, my son?

— Eh? Oh, I'm a city boy. I work down there for the country, for all of us. You know, this is excellent couscous.

— He knew the path well, Hajja took up again, smiling. (She was observing the chief. What held her attention more than anything was the crafty expression in his eyes: it explained, it seemed to her, the tortured deviousness of his language.) He had been taking this path for years, approximately once a week. He knew each stone, each hole. You know how our people walk? One eye on the sky, one on the ground, one looking left, the other right, and all the while even looking behind. Do you in fact have a name which your mother gave you at birth?

— Eh? What? replied the chief, dumbfounded. The name my mother... it's Mohammed.

— Like the Prophet?

— Yes, replied the chief. Yes, that's it. Like the Prophet.

The inspector's voice became child-like.

— Chief *Mohammed*. And I never knew it! Chief Mohammed.

— So you must be a man of peace, Hajja concluded, a man of your word, a man of honor. I am most content. This day is many times blessed: we have a man of goodness like the Caliph Ali in ancient times, and a man of honor, like the Prophet! There are men from the plains of pure heart after all, my goodness. Bourguine, bring the stew, and the watermelon.

— Right away, Hajja, replied Bourguine promptly.

— It's Allah's grace, exclaimed the inspector. What kind of stew, Hajja? Tell me now so I can look forward to it.

— A lamb stew with olives, dates, ginger. *Skenjbir*.

— Hajja, oh Hajja, said the inspector, tears in his eyes. I've never had it before, but I've often heard people talk about it.

— Relax, son, and eat. (She never took her eyes off the chief.) You're

47

keeping me from telling the story of Commander Filagare. And it's a long one. Very long. You see these torches burning around us? Well, they'll be burned down to the nubbins, and the story will not yet be finished. It will last deep into the night . . .

The peasant continued peacefully on his way, without a single care. He had just sold the two hens and the eggs. Coins jingled in the pocket of his *djellaba*, a whole fistful of them. He was barefooted, but he had donned his turban, like he did every time he went to the neighboring country where he could hang out at the train station, sitting on his haunches on the sidewalk, among all the passersby. He hadn't waited long: barely a couple of hours before he had sold his birds in the course of a long, happy, obstinate discussion on the harvest, the country, the family, and the high prices (of hens in particular); as for the eggs, he had sold those slowly, almost one by one. He had made sure he sat in a cool, well-ventilated corner so that the eggs were not spoiled by the heat.

Halfway between the train station and the mountain path, on a small, tarred road where the peasant was taking his time and surveying the clouds, a jeep suddenly pulled up behind him in a squeal of metal and tires. Two soldiers in camouflage netting the color of autumn leaves got out with their hands on their rifles.

— Hey, you over there!

The peasant stopped but didn't turn around. He waited.

— Your papers!

It was toward the end of the afternoon and some gray clouds were piling up to the east. But yonder where the home mountain lay, the horizon was clear. There couldn't therefore be any danger. He didn't quite understand what these men of war wanted from him, but everything would work out. He had come down from the *djebel*, sold his merchandise, and was on his way home. That's all there was to it. Surely these soldiers would leave him in peace. Which is why he turned around calmly and looked at them with neither fear nor affront, and stretched out his open hands to them, as proof of his good will.

— Where are you coming from? demanded the small, thick-set one who seemed to be in charge of the other, since it was he who appeared most nasty.

— Eh? replied the peasant, his mouth wide open.

— Are you deaf or what? Where did you just come from?

— Eh? repeated the old man.

And he smiled with a knowing air. He touched his ear with his index finger to show that he didn't understand a word of French.

— *Mnin tji?* shouted the other one in barracks Arab.

— Ah, replied the mountain man, finally understanding. *Nji filagare.*

At the very moment he uttered these rather simple and self evident words, the horror of war crashed violently down upon him.

A long time afterwards when he regained consciousness, he found himself

48

covered with bloody bruises and tied up with his own turban in the back of the jeep which was moving at high speed.

Still later, other soldiers in a cave, more blows, fists, boots, light more blinding than any August sun, barbarous voices which were more like cries and babblings, and innumerable and futile sufferings.

— He's a *fellagha*! He admits it, the son of a bitch!

— Where are the arms caches? You better talk!

— Where are the other filthy *fellaghas*?

— *Nji filagare!* said the peasant. *M'sieur, mon-z-ami, nji filagare.*

During the night, throughout the long hours until dawn, he continued to reiterate Allah's truth which, unhappily, was not man's truth: *"Nji filagare."* He was coming from the train station, he had gone there, he sold some hens to a brother, he didn't know his name, but he was sure he was a brother, a good fellow . . . the eggs? Oh, yes, to several brothers who spoke Berber or Arabic like himself . . . he didn't do anyone harm, he was tired and now the path which led to his mountain from which he should never have budged had he been able to read his fate in the sky, was long, but the sky in the west had been clear . . . And how, how, how, was he going to find the right way home?

And then there was peace, peace which arrived in the early morning hours along with a non-commissioned officer, and there was silence. There was an end to suffering and befuddlement, oh miracle and dignity of Allah. The officer had stopped and spoken to him in his own language, and what's more, he understood it. All would return to normal: the lizards back into their hole, the soldiers back to their war and he, the mountain man, he would retreat to his mountain where nothing ever happened except acts of Allah and nature. In his own language, everything became simple and elementary again, as shown by this superior Frenchman who, head cocked, actually listened. Yes, sir, he was coming from the train station, *"filagare"*. *"Fellagha?"* Who, him? Of course not, by Allah and the Prophet and the Christian de Gaulle, he was no *fellagha*. It was simply a human mistake, or an ink smudge—as the officer explained with a vicious glare to his men.

Nobody offered any excuses. No one had the courage—or the shame. But the peasant was allowed to pick up his money, on all fours, which was scattered beneath the torture table where he had undergone so many trials. It was merely aluminum, or a semblance of silver, nothing but cold metal, like the hearts of men when they've developed the minds of dogs. But it represented just fine the price of the flour and other commodities which he need to buy along the way for his family. He exited the cave backwards, hands pressed against his kidneys. He left slowly, with extreme deliberateness as if he had all the time in the world to photograph with his expressionless eyes each feature of each of these humans who had just dehumanized him.

For seven days and seven nights he slept in a cavern. Without eating or drinking. Like a bear in hibernation. Far from others, far from himself. The plaster which his wife made of leaves, ground roots, and a special clay did their job day after day on his feet, his fingernails, his neck, and his belly which was speckled with cigarette burns. But it was inside his head that a furrow had been plowed. And in this furrow a poisonous thistle was growing, higher and stronger every day, a sensation more violent than any he had ever felt before: vengeance. The roots of this thistle were hate, cruelty, and the urge to inflict death. A single seed was sufficient—a crippled word—to transform a simple peasant, born a good man, and good even into his old age, into someone who became in the weeks and months which followed: Commander Filagare.

He had no troops, not a single man. Even the fighters of the FLN (Algerian freedom fighters) thought for a long time that a tiger, thirsting for blood, stalked the land, from the mountains to the river valleys. And when they discovered his history via the "Arab telephone" they dubbed him Commander Filagare, and left him to wage his war, alone, and in the shadows. He was for them a merciless ally, a free-lance commando with no means of transport but a donkey, equally destitute, amorphous. He had no command structure, logistical support, or weapons: nothing but a simple knife with a bone handle which he would drive into mother earth after each use. He took no pleasure in killing, but he killed. It was necessary for him to cool down his heart before he could again become the son of the mountain, the man he once was.

He had known all the pathways and ravines, all the thickets and groves since childhood. A footprint, a broken branch, the smell of the air, the color of the sky, each stone, all were equally elements of his world. He knew them, and they knew him. It was a longstanding relationship. The slightest change could mean life or death. He had the perseverence of a rock, the patience of eternity. Seated all day long, immobile, old as the old stone wall against which he leaned, or perhaps protected by the shade cast by the mule who was as plant-like as his master, who would bother to notice this decrepit old man? And so the convoys would rumble by, heavy transports creaking and grinding in their passage, but nothing seemed to interrupt his lethargic reverie. They would shake him or kick him:

— Go on, get out of here.

They would throw stones at him.

— Beat it, scram! *Fissa!*

Without hurrying, smiling idiotically, he would mobilize his cracked and bare feet, go off and sleep a little further away. And the mule, switching his tail, would follow. And the old man, on occasion, could be most accommodating, volunteering information to the men of war, anything just to be left in peace.

— You seen the *fellouzes*?

— Eh?

— Arabs? *Fellaghas*?

— Ha! responded the peasant knowingly.

And he would slowly stretch out his arm, pointing to a spot on the horizon where he knew for sure the FLN had set up an ambush. He even once acted as a guide, donning a traitorous mien, and conducted a whole brigade to its destination: some abandoned camp where the soldiers would arrive at dusk and spend the night in wait for their enemy. They had planned for everything, except for the fleas which gave them no respite. At dawn, few of them were combat-ready! As for Commander Filagare, well, the night had swallowed him—and one mule looked like another. How could you fight a modern war in such a country, short of killing all the donkeys and leveling the mountains?

The Commander's knife did not gleam in the shadows: it was rusty. It was a night's bivouac, one lone man on watch. And when they came to relieve him, there was only a corpse, throat slit from ear to ear. The Commander would say to himself: one death a night, it's enough for my single vengeance. There were a good 360 days in a year. Sometimes more. At daybreak, somewhere between the mountain and the high plateaus, an old peasant slept with his mouth open, and a short distance away, an ageless, do-nothing mule. Once in a while he could manage to swat the flies away with his tail, but that was all. He would watch you go by, his large eyes framed by long lashes, with extreme commiseration as though you were the most pitiful of objects in his animal world. And here, there and all around scattered like little rock piles, idle, have-not peasants were sleeping also, identical in their earth-colored *djellabas*, their old age, and their petrified sleep. Other one-toed beasts stood motionlessly nearby, idlers all, as though testifying to the lethargy of a whole nation. And from one horizon to the other was barren, hostile earth where everything, the language, the customs, time itself, denied the 20th century.

And did Commander Filagare eat? No doubt. Mulberries and other berries collected in the scrub, leftovers begged from the garrisons, trash scavenged at dawn, roots carefully chewed with what remained of his teeth. Because of his age, his appetite was small. He needed so little to live! And besides, Allah was most great. He never let his creatures want, witness his "mule of the night" (as his master called him since he never slept at night) who would graze on anything, even the leaflets scattered by helicopter which invited the *fellagha* to "check their knives in the anteroom before sitting down to negotiate." Oh, yes, Allah certainly provided for man and beast, whether from the sky or the earth. Praise be to Him, most merciful and benificent! He gave life, and He added Filagare to the sum total of life on earth. Death was but the work of man. It was men who destroyed, and who bestowed death upon his fellows and upon the entire earth, not even missing the wheat or barley crops, which flamed with napalm under Allah's sun.

Filagare's gaze, sharp as a sparrowhawk's, ranged far and wide. From morning to evening, sitting there half-crippled, he photographed with his blank eyes both people and things, slowly, patiently, as though he were using an old bellows camera on a tripod. He had the time. He had all day. He took pictures which embraced the entire landscape. Then he would narrow his focus to the deeds and actions of a single man: *that* one was the most evil, and *he* would be his prey come nightfall. It was written! *Maktoub!* Commander Filagare could do nothing about it. It was Destiny. As the last rays of the sun seared the sky, he issued a brief order:

— Rrrrra!

And the "mule of the night" went into motion, calmly, off to accomplish his military task, known to him alone, ambling through the thickets, knocking over stones, smacking his four hooves upon the ground like a demon from hell, attracting attention, fear and bullets (but he knew how to run like the damned, and besides was protected by the grace of Allah)—yet for all that he was like a spirit sliding through the shadows, and he didn't miss his prey. Immediately afterwards, Commander Filagare would go to ground in some hole chosen beforehand.

With the death of each man, the peasant felt his heart grow a little colder, like a furnace slowly but surely using up its fuel. And there were the tears. As the chain of days, months and murders grew longer, he cried harder, more frequently. One could hear him in the distance and people would come to try and console him: Perhaps he had lost his children in the war and now he was an old orphan? Tell me, grandfather, did they burn your hut, light you meager harvest on fire, did they, in their madness, kill your sheep and your goats? They would recite the Canticle of Death in an attempt to console him, to remind him Islamically how infinitessimally small was man's place in creation: "Misery is ours, and our bodies shall surely perish. The sublime face of Allah is all that shall endure." Filagare would say not a word, hearing nothing and no one. His shoulders heaved convulsively, and he sobbed till he hardly breathed.

— Yes, said Hajja, smiling candidly at the Chief of Police. At his age he cried like a child, like a woman. Did you ever see your father cry?

— Who, me? replied the chief, disconcerted. (He suddenly wiped his mouth with the hemp bag which was his napkin.) No, I don't think so . . . I don't remember it ever happening.

— Aha! said Hajja.

She began to cut the watermelon in slices with a horn-handled knife. With her old head, used to the turning of the seasons and the passing of the years, she resembled nothing so much as a dry fig. You harvest them perfectly ripe, dry them in the sun, and string them one by one, in order of their readiness. Then you get a complete rosary of figs, more even if the fig tree is full of life and laden with fruit—unlike the one opposite the cavern. The poor thing is dead now, and the *scirocco* has scattered its ashes—or what remained of them. But Hajja remembered dried figs perfectly well just as she remembered all the little things throughout this long evening which were ordering themselves in her mind, some ripe, others still unformed and without precise meaning, fine details of only inconsequential interest. Quite casually, she had collected all this data from the chief's own mouth in an inoffensive little interrogation of which he himself had been unaware. She now knew who he was, his patronymic, what his father did, the ins and outs of his family, the quality of the wood in his office, the village where he was born, the city where he worked, why and how, the food he ate, his memories and thoughts which she had gone to such trouble to extract . . . she had reconstructed a whole life with little harmless questions which she had wrapped up in occasional asides during the course of her captivating tale of Commander Filagare.

Handing the chief of police a slice of watermelon, she said:

— Here, take it, my son.

— But why was this fellow crying, he asked?

— I don't know, she replied.

— You think maybe he was crying from chagrin? said the Inspector. Chagrin and remorse?

That one held no more secrets for her. He spoke before thinking. Too many over-ripe figs.

— I don't know, she repeated. No one has ever known.

— Well, announced the chief, I think I know. In fact, I'm sure of it. It jumps right out at you. You've simply got to have a brain in your head to understand what goes on in other people's minds.

And he didn't say any more. He was content to merely gaze around in the hope that someone else shared his opinion, if not his high intellect. He saw two attentive listeners: an adult who seemed to be dreaming of the wind, and a child whose eyes seemed to hold all the world's sadness. Inspector Ali gnawed patiently at his slice of watermelon, sounding something like a gurgling kitchen drain. Around them, the Ait Yafelman sat listening, grouped as one family. Nobody coughed, no one made the slightest comment. Hospitality was a sacred thing.

— The evidence is right there, said the chief in a resounding voice. He was proud of himself, that man. He, a simple primitive peasant, without, I'm sure, any education, none whatsoever, well, he became a commander through sheer hard work. By his own will power, he climbed to the top (or almost) of the military hierarchy, in other words, an institution duly established by the State.

— Oh, really? said Hajja. Eat your watermelon. It's delicious and cleans your insides. It's cool and calming.

Waving the slice of watermelon like a schoolmaster waving a pointer, carried away with enthusiasm, he elaborated on his thesis.

— He snapped the chains of poverty, misery and slavery. I am proud of him. That's my thinking, that's my feeling. He had the courage to stand up against the colonialists and he beat them . . . yes, he conquered them! Despite their weapons and all the forces of destruction at their command. He was crying with pride, with dignity, with self-sovereignty regained. I talk myself silly repeating to my assistants that if, in our so very beautiful country, everyone would think of the well-being of the State, everyone would be happy. It's as clear as the day.

The chief paused, hoping for a glimmer of interest on the part of someone in the audience who had at least some intelligence. But no one paid him any attention, and no one requested that he continue spewing forth words which in any case went right over their heads. Everyone avoided his eyes, with two exceptions: the child whose eyes were becoming sadder and sadder, and the adult who gazed at him with the fixed eye of a sole survivor. As for the inspector—his inferior, his direct subordinate, well, my word!—he was happily devouring the rest of his meal, as though it were the first in his life. Oh, patience, patience. Soon enough, tomorrow, . . . at the end of the official mission! . . . . "Patience and the passage of time are stronger than rage" as that French master of literature once said . . . La Fontaine . . . It was indeed that one, for the chief had learned his fables in elementary school, and he hadn't forgotten a single one.

— Surely, he started up again obstinately, this Filagare fellow must live in the capital. No doubt he has a residence appropriate to his status, and of course subordinates, and one of those limos with little flags flying from the hood. And that's only right! He should want for nothing since he is now receiving the fruits of his labor. He is someone, an excellency among all those Excellencies, a man of true merit. I'm sure I know him.

— I don't, said the inspector.

— Obviously, agreed the chief. You don't know *any* Excellencies, that's for sure.

— What I mean is that he's not listed in any of the index files. I have read them from A to Z.

— What are you talking about? Get your finger out of your nose!

— There's nothing about him in UNTEL, no Commander Filagare. Not a single card on him. Sorry. The official records are voluminous, as you well know. I've gone through them all. Nothing. Neither hide nor hair of any Commander Filagare. No trace. Not even on a Sergeant Filagare. Nothing about any first class private with the same name. Tell us, Hajja, what you told us was a legend, wasn't it? A nice story to enjoy the evening with, and spice up that beautiful meal which I'll never forget. That's it, isn't it, Hajja?

She gazed at first one, then the other of the two men from the plains, from down there. Then she clapped her hands.

— Bourguine!

— Yes? he replied.

— Put the peelings, and the watermelon rinds in that pail. This poor old mule is one of Allah's creatures, and he should share the feast. No, no, she said suddenly, leave the bones. They'll be good for soup tomorrow, Allah willing. And go bring Commander Filagare something to eat so he doesn't go to sleep on an empty stomach.

The chief seemed to suddenly become fatigued. The circles under his eyes became wider and darker, and the corners of his mouth sagged. He bleated out:

— Comm . . . the Commander . . . he's here? *Here?*

— There was nothing in the file, the inspector exclaimed, happily, immediately justifying his earlier certitude. There hadn't been the slightest piece of paper. So who was right? You or me?

— His name is Raho, said Bourguine. At least that's what we've always called him around here. I'll make a plate of couscous for him, OK, Hajja? And what else?

— Some dates, she immediately replied. And some chocolate. He likes the good things in life as well as anyone. Give him a whole bar. Who knows if there'll be any left tomorrow.

— Shall I bring him his knife?

— Absolutely. I'm sure he'll need it.

— But . . . but . . . , the Chief of Police was saying, but . . . that changes everything! I swear it, that changes everything!

Squatting on his haunches, arms resting on his knees, Raho contemplated the stars. Although they were far away, he knew that their light was hot. They swept away the shadows from the night, and from the hearts of men. They had been there since the beginning of the world, familiar and reassuring: Men did not live out their days in obscure solitude, oh no! What was enduring in life, the ancient belief in the four dominant elements, earth, fire, water and air, was passed down from generation to generation, across religions and cultures, as though all of man's enterprises were but a latticework through which was transmitted the ancient belief in the four dominant elements. All else was ephemeral. Man also was ancient, and remained so here on the mountain, down there on the plain, as well as in other lands belonging to the devil, or to Allah—ancient and earthbound, in the body, his passions, his needs, and even his ideas. He knew it. He was living witness to it.

These stars had been there in the sky from the first moment he had opened his eyes on this world, without doubt, those same timeless stars, each one

following its individual journey to some predetermined destination. They had guided his ancestors on their various wanderings, who, first pushed off the fertile plains into the high dry plateaus, finally huddled together on a little mountain, their last refuge. He, Raho, and what remained of an ancient people, had no more land to farm, had no more goals to strive for, no destiny on earth or in the heavens. The various conquerors and civilizers, of all races and languages, had forced their return to their original state, their condition at the dawn of time: denuded creatures, face to face with the elements. And perhaps, somewhere on the globe, maybe nearby, maybe very far away, there were other remnants of peoples like the Ait Yafelman, frozen in time. It was easy to accept his fate, as the cactus accepted the sandy soil in which it grew: You could consider poverty as life's fifth essential element. But why was there any hope?

Raho knew perfectly well that you couldn't get water to the lips of a man who was content to simply hold out his hands. Fine, but when someone gulps down huge quantities of hope and still finds his misery intact, implacable, waiting there at the end of all that hope, well, then it seems more atrocious than ever, and there's no way one can absorb it the way one once did, before. Raho, gazing at the stars, began to cry.

He remembered crying like that down in the country of the Algerians when he was Commander Filagare. He had been distressed at having had to kill Frenchmen, warriors perhaps, but men like himself, in order to regain his manhood. A little piece of his life was reborn with the death of each man.

And he had cried, surrounded as he was with the beauty of the sun, of the trees, the moon, the stars, the clouds, the splendor of life which made one's heart leap with joy.

And now, seated on the mountain in his sorrow, his gaze turned to the abyss of the milky way, Raho sobbed, his grief stretching from the sun, the mountaineer's star, all the way to the farthest sparklings of the celestial vault. These two urban dwellers who were assaulting his tranquility posed a mortal threat to the village—or, perhaps worse, to hope itself. Would he have to kill them?

With empty minds, and bellies stuffed like sacks of Kapok, they snored away, these two sons of the plain who knew only how to howl among humans. Which was what Bourguine was about to say in rather firm and resounding language when Hajja abruptly cut him off and said gently, in almost a whisper, that she had given precise instructions to Raho. For an instant, Bourguine stood there, motionless, with his mouth hanging open. Then he smiled and laughed long and silently. It was like a signal, far speedier than any communications satellite; the words of Hajja's order were transmitted to the four points of the compass, from Bourguine to the "Dictionary," and thence from one member of the Ait Yafelman family to another. The silver moon rose in the sky, surrounded by a coppery nimbus. It was witness to the joyful, but nearly silent conclaves which were taking place not only in the village but also in the surrounding villages, even as far away as the high plateaus where the towns had a veneer of a foreign civilization which had managed to modernize the ancient feudal ways—towns which were caught up in the close of the twentieth century.

Tomorrow, or the day after at the latest, Allah willing, the Ait Yafelman were going to hold a *diffa*, a truly ancient festival, with drums and with flutes. Raho had consulted the stars. He knew that Destiny followed the ancient Law with scientific exactitude.

5

The donkey woke up, standing on the mountain, at that time between night and what was soon to be dawn. Beneath him, between his four hooves, a light freshness rose from the earth. It wouldn't last long, just long enough to give a hint of dew. The days were becoming decidedly longer and more torrid than ever. There wasn't the slightest breath of air, not a single cloud in the sky. The day was dry as a thornbush. He couldn't do anything about it. That's the way it was. In other times, there had been rain in the sky and green grass underfoot.

Motionless, all his muscles relaxed, breathing very slowly, he absorbed the slight coolness rising from the ground, storing it in his body for the long day ahead. He had neither thoughts nor desires. One by one, the stars were bleached from the sky as the sun, born at a gallop, mounted its assault of the *djebel*, broiling the peaks. And, almost at the same time, it torched the red mule in successive waves of fire which rolled up from his tail to his ears, like a flood tide with the sun as it rises on the sea from the horizons to the shores. He folded his knees and allowed himself to collapse gently to his belly. Then, rolling onto his back, hooves stretched out in all directions, he gave his old hide a good, long rubbing, scraping it against the pebbly ground, one flank, then the other, his heavy head swaying in rhythm like a pendulum. At the very moment he was going to greet the god of light with a lusty bray, he saw his master prostrated toward the sun.

He had long known that he mustn't make any noise, not the slightest, when Raho was in that position, nor could he even cast his animal shadow between the man and that place high up on the mountain where the ball of fire was reborn every morning. Which is why he got back on his feet extremely gently, and stood there like stone with his eyes fastened upon his master. The sun became red, then whitened and flooded the sky, the earth, and time itself.

And the morning went this way: Raho stood up slowly, picked up his long walking stick, moved toward the donkey and smiled at him. He said:

— *Aji!*

He caressed his withers and repeated:

— *Aji! Yallah!* By the grace of Allah, come!

He grinned as he had many times before and the hand which was stroking him over and over again had become the hand of his companion. One ear flattened, the other pointed up to the sky like a minaret, the donkey didn't budge. He simply stood there staring at his master.

— But of course, said Raho in a peaceful voice. You and me, we're starting up again. So come on! *Yallah!*

The donkey picked up his front left hoof, then his rear left one and went into motion. His tail twitched with a kind of unutterable joy. He had aged since that distant time when he had romped like a demon in the land of the Algerians. But with an animal's instinct, he still knew the way.

The interrogation took place at two different times, and in two versions, differing somewhat according to rank: first, the chief's because he was the chief, responsible to his superiors who had preferred to entrust him with the official mission; then the inspector's, deemed prissy by the chief, and who after a hellish day filled with inane conversation, was rated 8.5 out of 20 in his notebook. Between the first question and the final response, the various elements of the investigation had piled up into an enormous heap of formless scraps of babble and nameless words. Time was born, it lived and died—and the chief, an officer of the police representing the State proceeded gradually or ex abrupto into various moods: from the innate respect which he normally accorded himself (and which others were obviously obliged to), to complete abandonment and surrender, passive discouragement, arms crossed in the face of destiny—not to mention the many stages between rage and despondency. But everything was scrupulously written down word for word by Inspector Ali, questions, answers, questions without any answers, the silences and sneers of illiterate peasants. At one point—11:18 to be exact—he noted when the chief, pushed no doubt to excess by some intractable peasant, nearly put a bullet in his subordinate's head.

For the arduous, special interrogation conducted by Ali (which could be described as Arab, or muslim, or perhaps primitive, even all of the above, and during which Ali had to repeat several times wearily to his chief, "you have to do what you have to do, chief, let me get on with it", no fewer than three regulation sized notebooks were required. The Chief of Police had been forced to play the role of scribe during all this, and he duly wrote down what he heard, including the inspector's questions which leaped around to every conceivable topic, as well as the responses which he elicited, some disconcertedly direct, others lengthy, tedious and full of excess verbiage.

It had all commenced with a vibrant awakening at the regulatory 7:30 a.m. set off by the chief's quartz watch alarm whose little electronic vibrations resounded off the walls of the cavern: beep-beep-beep . . .

— What on earth is that? said the chief, waking up with a start. Then he realized where he was, and what it was. He didn't say: "By Allah, what am I doing here?" but he certainly thought it. He did *not* throw his wristwatch against the cavern walls. When necessary, he knew how to control himself. And anyway, it was a highly perfected gadget, absolutely symbolic of his own degree of evolution. With a civilized index finger, he pressed the button which read "alarm off" and the electrons became silent, as if by magic. In truth, it was that simple.

His mouth open, exposing his oversized front teeth, Inspector Ali stretched out on his animal hide bed and continued to snore peacefully. This son of the root of a dog's tooth must be truly dense, thought the chief. With his lips pursed, he let out a whistle. He then whistled more loudly, with authority. He shouted:

— Wake up!

He jabbed the inspector sharply in the ribs and roared:

— Get up! Every morning . . . every single morning it's the same old thing. I've got to do everything myself in these barracks!

Inspector Ali opened his eyes, first one, then the other, and gazed at his chief as if he were seeing him for the first time. He started to stand up and, with his right hand balanced between his legs, got up stiffly as though he were suffering from sciatica. A moment later, right outside within earshot, there was a sound akin to loud radio static: first off there was a steady stream of liquid under pressure; then a series of regular, detailed interruptions and finally, irregular splurts. As the inspector came back in, he was absently blotting up the last drops with his *djellaba*. He said:

— Yes, chief, what's goin' on?

— You pig! screamed the chief.

— Really, chief? What do you do? Don't you have your needs?

The chief stood up heavily.

— Wait for me here. I'll return in 30 seconds.

He went out and came back a quarter hour later with his face in a tight grimace. He asked:

— Did you hear anything?

— No, chief, nothing. Really.

— I'm no pig. When I have 'needs' as you call them, I attend to them silently. Naturally.

— Yes, but for me it was urgent, chief. By Allah and the Prophet, I swear it!

— Leave Allah out of it, the chief cried out. Don't be blasphemous.

— But, chief, it was com . . .

— Fine, I understand. Don't go on about it. And stop scratching your balls.

— Yes, chief. I'll follow your orders. What should I do now? What's the itinerary?

— You can start by getting dressed and going to look for my uniform. I'm vulnerable, diminished in these cretin clothes. My superiors wouldn't recognize me, I promise you. Go find my uniform instead of standing there yawning.

— Where?

— Wherever you want, you idiot. Wherever it is now. You're a police inspector, aren't you? Has your brain gone soft with all that garbage you stuffed into yourself last night?

— Aha! exclaimed the inspector. His face brightened immediately. That was a real Pasha's feast. It only lasted so long, but all things must come to an end. Ahh, I'll remember that tagine stew through the times of lean and plenty. It sure doesn't compare to the chickpea soup my good wife made. Not by a long shot. Believe me, chief, I'm telling the truth. It was good! I'm going to divorce her as soon as I return home.

— Go find me that uniform! howled the chief, his face crimson with rage at 7:58 in the morning. Find it or I'll kill you on the spot!

— With this very step I'm going, chief. Don't get mad. And he exited muttering something about breakfast.

And then there was the second episode concerning the uniform in question. Oh, now, it was quite clean and dry, spread out in the sun on a bush. But it was missing all its buttons. Beautiful yellow copper buttons which Hajja had taken off to create a pair of gleaming bracelets. Storming about at the entrance to the cavern holding his pants up with both hands, the chief had run out of words to express his indignation. Both his French and his Arab vocabularies were exhausted. He was speechless. Unruffled, the inspector transformed himself into a diplomatic negotiator, going back and forth between the man without buttons and the old woman bent over the ground looking for twigs and brambles with which to light her fire.

— The chief thinks, Hajja, that during the night, a *djinn** popped the buttons off his uniform and transformed them into those bracelets around your wrists.

— It wasn't a *djinn*, it was me. They're pretty, aren't they? They look like serpents' eyes.

— Yes, indeed, Hajja, they're pretty, but . . .

— Here, you see that rope lying over there? I'll give it to you. He can hold his pants together with it.

— He'd never go for it, never.

— Oh, yes, absolutely! All he has to do is tie a knot. As for the jacket, it's not worth closing it. It's going to be very hot, my son. That way, it'll be fine.

Twenty or thirty meters away, the chief stood waiting for the results of the negotiations. With each step the inspector took towards his chief, he contemplated how to turn the negative facts into cheery probabilities. The sun was already high in the sky, and it was imperative to avoid the slightest risk of conflagration.

*Genie

— It's this way, chief: As sure as zero plus zero makes zero, that woman from the Middle Ages doesn't have your brains. She nicely washed your official uniform and then . . . now, don't go making fun of her, chief, calm down. Well, so: she had this silly notion that you can't very well wash buttons, so she took them off, shined them, and even scented them. They are now drying around her wrists. They're in good hands, believe me! Good for us, too, otherwise any passing peasant would've swiped them, dry or not—or some crow swooping out of the sky. You know it!

Two or three minutes later, he said:

— That was a good idea she had, wasn't it, chief?

— I've had enough! You're off your rocker. You're bananas! A goner! You're not accomplishing anything. Don't say a single word to this woman. Just go over there and bring back my buttons. Period! That's an order! Carry it out!

— Fine, chief, that's just what I would say . . . concluded the inspector as he retraced his steps. Trudging back along those twenty or thirty meters, the two elements consisting of the chief's opposition to his plea bargaining and the old woman's little caper transmuted into an algebraic formula with two unknowns laden with emotions and memories.

— As you, in your wisdom and experience, figured out, that man is nothing but a poor orphan, even though he comes from the city. When his father died, his entire patrimony consisted of a few worthless pieces of copper: Indeed those very buttons.

— Aha?

— Yes. It's sad, but that's life. And in memory of his dead father (Allah rest his soul) he had that yellow metal fashioned into buttons by an artisan. And because of his fondness for his father, he had those buttons sewn on to his uniform. In that way, even beyond death, father and son are united.

— Really? Is that true?

— Yes. So here's what we're going to do, Hajja. Open your ears as well as your large heart: You return to him his funerary memorabilia and I will give you a beautiful pair of bracelets. See?

— Hmmm! said Hajja. Hmmmm! They look something like a fox trap. I'll give them to Raho.

— If you like, said the Inspector. Certainly, if you prefer. And if you ever trap one of those old foxes, save me a piece of meat from the thigh. I've heard it's very good, especially if you cook it in its own glandular juices.

He had to explain to her how the handcuffs worked, using one syllable words. He warned her about a certain devilish police practice which could cause the steel to snap shut on you.

— Whatever you do you mustn't put both bracelets on at the same time, otherwise, zap! it's all over, and there's no way to get out of them, especially with both hands locked up. Do you understand, little mother?

— Here, Hajja, he concluded. Here are the keys just in case. And he went off to sew the chief's buttons back on starting with the pants. The chief fidgeted the whole time, squirmed like a politician reviewing his options and

63

waved his arms about spasmodically. And the things he said! ... But the inspector shut his ears and worked the needle and thread dextrously. And he was amazed he managed not to prick his boss in some roll of fat, particularly the belly which was very large. Probably through the grace of Allah. The sun had already reached its first quarter station in the sky and its rays were sharp. That's why once all the buttons were sewn on again under his close scrutiny, the chief took off his jacket, folded it carefully, mopped his brow and said:

— It's hot.

He pulled out his shirttails and flapped them back and forth like a fan. Then he said determinedly:

— OK. Let's not waste time. We've got to get on with this investigation, particularly since I can't count on you. Time flies, and you're playing seamstress. What about our official mission?

— You're right, chief. Unless I'm wrong, three minus 3/4 equals 2 1/4.

— What are you talking about? What are you calculating? Has the heat melted your brain?

— Absolutely not, replied the inspector with simple certainty. It's not the heat. I've been used to it since childhood because of my father's oven. Let me explain: Usually, hospitality lasts three days. We've been here since midday yesterday, which makes 18 hours, or three fourths of a day, if you prefer. So, we have two and a quarter days left. Right? And we haven't yet had breakfast.

The chief turned this over carefully in his head and said:

— Go find me a chair.

— What chair? asked the inspector. I've got good eyes, and I don't see any chair around. We're in the country, after all.

— So what's that mean?

The chief's tone of voice was dry, cutting, glacial, and was clearly intended to transfix his interlocutor on the spot.

— Oh, well, said the inspector with a certain commiseration, there's nothing but that old crate. A long time ago, it probably had soap from Marseille in it. Most likely 14 to 18. That was the First World War. Our country had just been placed under protection. I gotta tell you, chief, that old soap worked real well, lots of lather ...

— Bring me this seat, and stop talking gruel and pablum.

— Yes, chief.

— Over here, closer, so I can see our suspects. They must be in the light and I in the shade.

— We should have brought a searchlight.

— What, and electricity too?

Seated, the chief scuffed his feet on the ground, blew through his mouth, then took out a mechanical pencil from his pocket and twirled it between his fingers. The inspector could see that this little gesture helped restore the chief's confidence. The mechanical pencil had been on its twelfth rotation when the inspector decided to ask a question:

— What do we do now, chief?

— You don't do anything. You follow orders. You carry them out. Period. In the meantime, I will reflect on matters and proceed with the investigation from start to finish. It will be instructive for you, nurture your growth.

— OK, chief. Working with you is one of the gifts of Democracy.

— All citizens are useful, the chief went on. All professions. But you have to indeed remember that there are differences, enormous differences, between one socio-economic category and another. The factory worker goes to his factory and works there all day long. But it's mindless work. He works mechanically, right? He simply carries out his tasks. And what does a professor do in his scholarly establishment? He inculcates in his students knowledge, education, culture and civic responsibility. But . . . but, in fact he had at his disposal books and manuals in which everything is written down in black and white. He reads them, that's it. Take for example the deputies, and even the ministers. You would think they direct the policies of the State. Not at all. Not in the slightest. They only carry out directives which come from on high. Because luckily for us there's someone on top who does the thinking—way on top. The head of our civic body!

— Oh, yes, agreed the inspector with intense veneration. May Allah bless and protect him.

— Even the ministers and the big-shots! Oh, I'm not saying that they don't think, but only half the time, 50%. Believe me, little fellow, rare are those who have the cerebral faculties to really think, cogitate and conceptualize. I'll give you an example: an investigation—I mean, a superior investigation like the one the government has entrusted me with, now that's something! It is very, very difficult because I have nothing to go on: we're starting from zero, absolutely nothing. I have to work my brain and bring the investigation to a close as the captain guides his ship in a storm-tossed sea. And if I want to reach a successful conclusion, occasionally I must break it down into four distinct steps, like the four movements in a classical symphony. Do you know what a symphony is?

— *Bitouven*? tried the inspector.

— *What?* said the chief, suddenly finding himself brutally at the bottom of Mount Sinai.

— *Clockwork Orange*, something I saw at the movies. Dynamite! Lots of blood. They played the music of this *Bitouven* I mentioned.

— Allah in heaven! intoned the chief.

His eyes were black and agitated, like satellites wobbling madly in their orbits—the kind of eyes that have never attained satisfaction, and never would.

— Let's see now, he began philosophically. You are a member of the State's police force?

— Yes, chief, no doubt about that.

— And you are indeed an inspector?

— Yes, chief, I have my I.D. and my badge.

— Your name is Ali?

— That's right. It always has been...I've never changed it. No pseudonym, no 007 like that chap in the movies, James Bond. This isn't the movies. *Police-police, camarades après, moi.*

— You have carried out, under my direction, several investigations—fairly routine ones, wouldn't you say? Trifling matters, second rate events?

— Seventeen arrests, chief, and a fellow who croaked in my hands. I must say that he had a fragile neck, that bastard ripped from his mother.

— And I covered for you at the time for that asinine fatality. You were acting in the line of duty. But let's get back to our little piece of business: Are you quite sure you don't have a twin?

— Yes, chief, I'm quite sure. There's no twin brother in my file, which you yourself have carefully gone over in the past.

— You wouldn't perhaps have a double who could have taken your place, some big jerk who is here right now, clowning around, before my very eyes, while his chief is attempting to elevate the tone of the conversation?

— Oh, *that*? exclaimed the inspector. He spat on the ground. You see, I was kidding. That's all, chief. It's awfully hot, and a few odd words slipped out of my mouth. I couldn't help it. Now what were you saying?

The chief stubbornly kept silent while the sun rose ever higher in its conquest of the sky. What must be, must be: some countries developed, and others underdeveloped, so far behind, in fact, that it was difficult, almost superhuman, to achieve any progress, however small... inasmuch as the industrialized countries weren't going to wait for them! But Allah is greatest—despite the modern government currently running the State...

Looking at the dangerously inscrutable face of his chief, the inspector shifted from foot to foot, feeling indecisive, the way he was when he had to go to vote. The political process reached him in the form of similar and virtually interchangeable voting papers, each with almost the same platform and same words. So how to make a good decision? It was so hard to choose—as hard as obsidian. Vote for the UNTEL party which advocated national independence, respect for the country's institutions and social progress? Sure, why not? But there was yet another UNTEL party which claimed advocacy for social progress, respect for the institutions and national unity!... It was all the same, the institutions were still in the middle, immovable, all by themselves for pete's sake—perhaps it was just a matter of how you cut it—this independence, this social progress had simply swapped places. Did that necessarily mean there was a change in the choirmaster? By Allah, but it was difficult to avoid an error in judgment which could possibly result in the collapse of the constitutional monarchy! If only there weren't these stupid ass elections!... In the days of the French, you simply didn't vote. It was easier. There wasn't this tension which weighed on the brain and inflamed the blood. "Most mighty Allah, most merciful and benificent, King of creation and of the last Judgment, speak to me! Breathe the right answer... the color of the voting card, at least...?

A hand pulled aside the curtain of the voting booth and tapped on the shoulder of the inspector.

— Heh, fellow, there's a line out there. Get it over with! Get over your false pregnancy. It's not worth waiting until the ninth month.

Occasionally, they almost had to forcibly march him out of there, and it didn't help matters any to display his police I.D. to his colleagues who were keeping an eye on the polling station and the vote counters. "Heh, be a sport, pal," he'd say to them holding out his voting card. "Why don't you vote in my place? I've got to get back on the beat, I'm in a rush. Heh, and thanks a lot, OK?"

Here, in the cavern, facing his chief who was evaluating him with his little black questioning eyes, how should he vote? There was no colleague, no one, to whom he could delegate his responsibility. For the rust on a nail, for a half-yes or a quarter-no, this chief, who was but one of untold legions of chiefs, could easily deprive him of his daily bread and sack him. At any time, he could write out a report on him, and affix his finicky signature above the official seal. This duly officialized report would engender a slew of chiefly signatures and seals, each one covering for the preceding one and . . . The inspector preferred not to think about it. He loved life. Opting for the pure and simple suspension of his personality, he said:

— Chief, I've just been kicking myself in the rear because I deserve it. My behavior is unspeakable—always fooling around and interrupting you with asinine comments. If I were you, I'd be permanently pissed off, alas! That's the way I'd feel about it. When I think how you, chief, an educated, learned man, cultivated and intelligent, what's more, pulled me off the playing fields of misery, one gray, cursed day, me kicking a ball around because I had nothing better to do, . . . when I think about it, tears spring to my eyes. I was in rags except for the soccer togs on my feet . . .

— Shoes, said the chief. Not togs. Speak correctly.

— Yes, chief, sad little shoes which didn't even belong to me. Hunger was gnawing a hole in my belly, since all I had had was soup and some crusts of bread. I had nothing, I was nothing, nothing at all! And then I entered the police force where you were, and from on high, you kept an eye on my career, all the way from that lofty position which you occupy. Three years ago, you had the generosity, the goodness of heart, to get me to take that exam which allowed me to ascend to the enviable rank of inspector—an exam which I'll remember for the rest of my life . . .

— That's right, said the chief. He was beginning to smile but then his face suddenly hardened. Your dictation was deplorable. But you were a good shot.

— You knew how to lighten up the century old shadows in my brain . . . May Allah protect you and keep you in good physical and mental health. One day, I was in the sentry box of the Central Commissariat, standing guard like a dog—I mean an oak—from morning 'til night, the next I found myself in an office seated in an armchair like a pasha—I who had never sat on anything but the ground like my father and all my people. And I had at my disposal a telephone with all kinds of buttons. You taught me how to use it.

— An American telephone. The best, said the chief. When you're with the

State's police, you got to have what you need . . . no old dial phone, just highly sensitive touch-tones. As you well know, in our profession you have to act fast. To the slightest summons from up above.

— Yes, chief, and there's lots of that! But you've done much more for me. You've taught me all the nuances and skills of the profession, especially how to beat out the other police officers. And by Allah, that's something! You instructed me in that art of studying dossiers, showed me how to read them, and interpret them almost down to the last comma! And that's important since almost all words, to start off with, are suspect.

— Oh, no, the chief protested gently. Only some are suspect. You know the difference, don't you?

— Not completely, admitted the inspector, but with your help, I'll get the hang of it. I just don't understand why you continue to take the trouble to hoist me up to your level. Bringing me up to your intelligence, making me an adjunct worthy of the name, capable of listening to each word you say and carrying out your orders. You know, though, chief, some of your words are just too . . . too vast for my comprehension.

— Let's not exaggerate, said the chief, unbuttoning the belt to his pants. Let's just say that some of them are too dense.

— That's it, chief, you've found the exact word: as dense as a thick fog. And what I mean by that is: my brain, unlike yours, doesn't manage to pierce the fog. Do you understand? And then, just earlier, you were attempting to

68

explain to me the high principles which will guide you through this mission, things which I know nothing about . . . and instead of listening very attentively to you, . . . well, by Allah and the Prophet, I deserve to be knocked around.

And with the back of his hand, he gave himself a magisterial slap across the face.

— Why do you behave that way, Inspector Ali? he said, speaking out loud to himself. Do you think you're feeling the burden of your past? You know, anything is possible in this country. As I've told you a thousand times, my father was a poor bake-shop caretaker. I've already told you about my grandfather, haven't I? No? Well, he was only a tradesman. Had what he needed, but no more. And they tell me that before him, my forefathers were simple peasants with no history. They had nothing but fifteen or twenty hectares per family. Oh, hardly more. No comparison with the big landowners today who have tens and tens of thousands of hectares . . . those landowners really count—they're obviously people to reckon with. No, a hundred times no, my miserable ancestors had just enough to live on: grain, milk, livestock, chickens, some horses. Do you see the picture, chief? I'm the sad product of that whole line of barefoot peasants. As deep into the virgin genealogical forest you care to penetrate, there's not a single outstanding personality.

— I'm beginning to understand, remarked the chief pensively. One of these days I'll explain to you what they mean when they talk about the dawning of human consciousness and evolution.

— Well, I'm thanking you in advance, chief. According to what I've been told—old wives tales, legends and stuff—back in the days of those Andalousian Arabs there were a couple of intellectual types who were wind bags. Ha! They drew maps of countries and oceans. You see what I mean? It seems there were even some who wrote silly little books. So you see where I'm coming from? Not a single police chief or soldier in my family. Not even a simple cop.

— Don't be sad, my brother, said the chief. You're in the police now. So think of your children. Their path is all laid out. The hope is there. Horizon 2000!

— Yes, chief. But I can't stop thinking about my origins and what do I find? Do nothing ancestors. Chief, you've picked up a big zero. Me. I'm perfectly aware that you can't turn a zero into three or four. Or even two, should we say. It's the mantle of the Middle Ages which weighs on me and holds me back.

He paused and sighed. The chief had unbuttoned his shirt a long time ago and was in the process of unlacing his boots. A stripe of sun entered the grotto, fiery as a white hot sword. The chief said in his school-masterly tone:

— It is right and normal from time to time to critique oneself in order to understand the foolishnesses in us. That's what you've just done. That's good. It's very good, in fact. By doing thus, you've held yourself up to question. You've seen yourself. You've undertaken your own investigation. An

examination of yourself. Little by little as the bird builds his nest you will end up by evolving through the recognition of your basest faults and your blemishes. Bound to happen. That's what you call progress. Even more important, you must listen to your elders.

— I'm listening to you, chief.

— Not always. Not always! I very much want to help you evolve to whatever extent possible, because, believe me, I wish you well. I can indeed envisage your future and try to make it as easy for you as sticking a finger into a patty of butter. Because, who knows? . . . Today an inspector, tomorrow, deputy chief, maybe.

— Oh, chief!

— And later, probably much later, who knows . . . chief!

— Oh my God!

— In the meantime, help me take off my boots. My feet are boiling and my mind has to be relaxed before I can tackle my mission.

— Sure, chief, absolutely. You can't let that get heated up.

One after the other, the boots echoed against the grotto walls as they fell to the ground.

— As I was saying earlier at the beginning of the discussion—a *briefing* in American—I will divide this investigation into four movements. Firstly, I'm going to . . . hold on, I'm going to entrust my special pen to you. Don't bust it! I'm counting on you.

— Never fear, chief. It's a great honor . . .

— It's a TK-Matic. It can go through a thousand meters of writing before you have to reload it. Can you imagine that? A thousand meters—a kilometer even.

— By Allah and the . . .

— Do you have your notebook?

— Yes, chief. Here it is. I hardly dare write with this marvelous instrument.

— Dare. Note down what I'm going to say to you. So, first movement: I'm going to behave like there's no big deal, chat with these peasants about this and that, the rain and the good weather, the sowing and the harvest, all with a view to gaining their trust, because you know, aside from the patch of ground they stand on you could shoot them all and be none the poorer. Second movement . . . Are you taking notes?

— Yes, chief. This thing moves all by itself in fourth gear. I can hardly stop it, so continue.

— Secondly, I will delve into their psychologies—in other words, get into their thick skulls. I'll rummage around a little here, a little there, and in no time at all, I'll figure out the one basic thing I need to know: who's a suspect and who isn't. Although these clods may try to stick together . . . well, trust me. Third movement: I isolate the suspects into a separate group and from there . . . I radically change the whole tone of the investigation: Last name? First name? Profession? Police record? Leisure time? Alibi?

— Just like the Commissariat?

— That's right. But in greater depth. You have to take the circumstances into account since I'm not in my office. Fourth and last movement: I find suspect number one, he becomes the guilty one, and I take him in. Our work is then finished, and the mission accomplished.

— How long will it take, chief?

— That depends . . . that depends . . . One day, two days, everything depends on the circumstances. Why do you ask me that? Are you in a rush to get back home and see your lovely wife?

— Me? Me? cried the inspector. Allah forbid! Don't talk to me about that old bag. I had to come all the way here to find out what real food tastes like. We didn't have any breakfast this morning, chief. I suppose these beggars only have one meal a day, if they can find it.

The chief began to laugh. It was a benevolent, paternal laugh.

— I've seen to everything, you snail brain. Over there, in my bag. Biscuits, sandwiches. A thermos full of coffee. And some silverware.

— Sounds like heaven.

— Leave that bag alone. In a little bit. Write! Educate yourself. Earn your future bars by the sweat of your stomach.

— Yes, chief.

— Write: . . . the four movements of the investigation will have four different tonalities. First off, inoffensive familiarity, anything goes. Little by little, I modulate it . . . progressively, right? In little stages until the tone becomes neutral, precise and functional. Next scene, the volume increases, amplifies right up to the point where I will separate the wheat from the chaff and single out the suspects. Finally, when the guilty one stands there before my very eyes, I revert to my true tone—that of truth, truth which has motivated me

71

from the very beginning of this investigation. As you can see, it's really quite simple. But you have to understand the vagaries of human nature. Close your notebook and give me back my mechanical pencil.

— Here you go, chief. If only I had had this machine in primary school . . .

— What's this? What *is* this? yelled the chief. This sticky stuff? I swear I can't trust you with anything. You bungle everything. I'm sick and tired of you. That's what comes from eating with your fingers, like you did last night! I loan you a costly, precision instrument and what do you give back to me? A revolting, dirty, greasy, slippery mechanical pencil! Haven't you washed your hands yet?

He began to rub the TK-Matic with his handkerchief, carefully wiping it off. The inspector looked sadly at his hands. He said very simply:

— There's no more water.

— What do you mean, no more water? What kind of excuse are you trying to hand me? Do you think you can get out of it like that?

— No, chief. Such a dishonest thought wouldn't occur to me. Let me explain: earlier when I was chatting with Hajja about those buttons, I learned that there wouldn't be any tea. And so no breakfast, at least not until the picnic you've got in your satchel. That's why my stomach is rumbling right now.

The chief clipped the mechanical pencil on his uniform pocket, looked his handkerchief over, rolled it into a ball and threw it off into a corner as far from himself as possible. Then with his forehead creased into a furrow of incomprehension, he said:

— You've come up empty handed. I've had more than enough of you. What's this mixed up story: sticky fingers, tea and incongruous innard noises?

— You see, chief, keep calm. Don't fly off. It's Hajja. She told me yesterday that there was a reserve of water, of about three or four gourdsful, for the rest of the week. And then we arrived, and you drank a little. You refreshed yourself. More than a little, shall we say. Then they had to cook this whole big, beautiful meal. With water, obviously. Three gourdsful minus three leaves us with three empty containers. Not a single drop left. Conduct your interrogation carefully. Hajja admits there's a well down below, see? But it's a dozen kilometers through that blast furnace outdoors. That's what the old lady told me. She added with a smile that the neighboring villagers continually draw from this well, one after the other. To such an extent that right now . . . well, you can imagine the situation. Hajja's eyes looked honest when she imparted to me this last bit of information. I don't at all doubt her word. She lives here. Not I. Not you, chief. It's the beginning of the end as that big, fat fellow—Churchill was his name—used to say.

The inspector swallowed his saliva and fired off his final thought:

— It's a calamity.

Several minutes passed slowly by with the rhythm of a leaky faucet. The chief's furrowed brow changed color from mauve to violet due to the intensity of his reflections. When he opened his mouth it was to issue one dry order:

— I don't give a damn! Wash your hands. Figure it out. I bet your notebook is also covered with grease.

— OK, chief. As the soldiers say, wartime is wartime.

The inspector spat resolutely onto his hands and rubbed them together as if he were using soap. There was always the chief's handkerchief over in the corner, but he refrained from touching it. He took a long time wiping his fingers on the sheep skin that he was sitting on, taking special care with his finger nails. He examined his hands against the light, sniffed them, and upon thinking it over, said:

— They're clean chief. I think. If there is no more water, please allow me to ask with the deepest respect and solicitude: what's going to happen to us? Here we are, fine and dandy in this hole like a couple of rats dying of thirst— and, soon enough, hunger. There's no miracle forthcoming, except the little picnic in your satchel. But it won't last long. How much is a thermos? Hardly enough to humidify one's gullet, being at the edge of death as we are. I'm already running out of saliva, and I'd do well to shut up. Do you see that sun, chief? It's heating up. It's not going to stop heating up. I, the son of my father, born and bred in an oven, I almost fainted a little while ago when I was out there chatting with Hajja. Do you want to find out for yourself, chief? Hunh?

The crease in his forehead had disappeared, and in its place, an intelligent smile illuminated the face of the chief.

— No, he replied categorically. I won't get talked into that. It's not worth it. There are more noble tasks before me which require all my mental faculties. I don't have time to fool around with you. Instead, help me pull over my seat. This fiendish sun is blinding me. It would serve me right if I lost my sight.

— Yes, chief, that would be a catastrophe. Let's not say any more about this minor detail.

The inspector pushed his boss, who remained seated on the box, with all his might.

— What detail?

— Water.

— Oh. Good, said the chief. Hmmmm! Listen carefully. No, no, it's not worth writing down. Economise on paper. I am delegating to you right now a rogatory warrant. Go find me these peasants, everyone of them. I'm going to really and truly start this investigation. They're certainly going to laugh. You've dallied long enough.

— All of them at the same time? asked the inspector. How will they all fit into this hole?

The chief exploded.

— I said "*tous tant qu'ils sont.*" That means, in every language in the world, "one after the other right up until the last." You lab specimen! Don't twist my words. Go find the accused in order of importance: the biggies first, like Hajja, Commander Filagare, certainly Bourguine, then the middling ones, and finally the small fry.

— I'm off! (But he didn't make any preparations to leave.) And if you were to interrogate them in order of declining importance, chief? Start with the finger, and the arm will be dragged into the gears, followed by the shoulder, the neck, and finally the head and all that. It's simple. First things first, as the Chinese say.

— Are you going or not?

— Right away, chief.

Inspector Ali took care not to move: and for good reason. In front, he faced human obtuseness, but behind, there was an even greater danger: the furnace. In lava-like flows the sun entered triumphantly into the cavern. The walls had begun to steam. And there were still two days of hospitality left!

— I have a better idea, he said. Let me outline it briefly to you, chief. It goes as follows: First, we sprint out of here; second, we take off as fast as possible in our car, all the windows down; third, we stop at the first hotel we come to so we can freshen up, and have a snack and then, if it comes to that, by the time we get back here, it'll be the end of summer. When things get complicated, it's best to take a philosophical view, and let them drop. The French claim that you must do something in such cases, but we're not French, are we, chief?

— Consider me as your brother, inspector. Take all the time you need to answer this little question: Should I make out a report on you now, or when we return to the capital? Choose. Defend yourself. Give me your arguments for and against. Imagine that you are before a judge who is very sympathetic to you, who has tried to help you, but can do no more, he's up against a stone wall. *Merde!*

— I agree.

— You agree to what?

— I'll go search out the guilty ones, chief. Immediately. Could I have a gulp of coffee from the Thermos?

— Did I have anything to drink?

— No, chief.

— Am I thirsty?

— I wouldn't know.

— So?

— So fine, no coffee. By Allah, we won't say another word about it. He exited slowly, shrugging his shoulders at what might come. If he was thinking of anything, it was of the gun which the Chief of Police had forgotten the night before in his anger, near the enclosure where Raho stood like a sentinel.

The red donkey ambled along eastward under the burning sun. He didn't hurry.

— *Sire, yawlidi!* his master had said to him. Move on, my son. I am putting this man in your care. Take him to the place you know.

74

The man in question had been astride his back since dawn, with neither a saddle nor bridle, balancing himself to the rhythm of the slow trot, and the occasional jolt, and his feet were almost grazing the ground. On the mountainside, the path was very steep and narrow, bordered by brambles and ravines which were so steep in places that the mule had a hard time discerning how to proceed. But he stretched out his hocks, carried all his weight on his rear hooves, and turned with the path. He had to take great care with his human cargo, and serve as his guide—and his eyes.

Way off in the distance, as comforting as the voice of a friend, the raspy intermittant sound of a bull's horn beckoned. With his eyes angled up behind him, the donkey strained to hear the slightest variations in the call's resonance. But with each step he moved farther from the sound of the horn. The sun seemed to be descending, turning time to liquid, and soon there was no sound other than the hammering of his hooves against the stony soil.

6

About an hour after his departure, or two or three according to the chief who was at the end of his patience, and his soliloquy, Inspector Ali returned, preceded by a sort of aura. He negligently carried his civvies under his arm, rolled up in a ball around his shoes, and, wearing *babouches* on his feet, he was draped in a Saharan *gandoura*. His carriage radiated pride. He had a fierce allure, lean, parched and rebellious. If he had eased his hunger and thirst during the course of a rambling conversation with a peasant who had become his friend under the July sun, he made sure not to mention it. You gotta do what you gotta do, but you *don't* have to do what you *don't* have to do! Glancing at the chief, he laid his clothes in a corner of the grotto and said most diplomatically:

— Here I am, chief. My goodness, but these synthetic fibres are comfortable—in America, or Italy, or Paris, and maybe in some of our own more highly evolved cities. But here in the land of the Middle Ages, they're worthless against the sun. One of the Ait Yafelman who was passing by sold me this desert *gandoura* for a few coins. For three times nothing, really. When I think of the *Klebs Mediteranee* tourists who buy those folklore products for huge wads of bills! So, I therefore enlisted the dolt for the rogatory commission which . . .

— Report! interrupted the chief.

He expressed this one word emotionlessly. Anger had had the time to rise and ebb during these hours when all authority had found itself holed up in the cavern, run up against the worst of obstacles: solitude. The unemployment, the idling of power. Yes, by now he had swallowed his fury along with the bile and the gall. Everything was classified, detail by detail, in a fat file stored deep in his memory. He had made his decision and it was irrevocable. But later . . . later, in a day or two when this mission . . .

● ● ●

— Where are the suspects? he asked in an even voice, as limp as his plastered down hair.

Upon hearing these almost friendly words, the inspector immediately sensed danger. That's why, inspired by governmental presentations on television, he painted an idyllic picture of the economic and social situation, based on the principle which had faced the tests of both fire and water: 1) Everything is fine, and 2) Things would be better if the rise in petroleum products . . ., etc.

— Everything's going fine, chief. During the course of my duties, I was able to stand up to the sun. You have to do what you have to do, since orders are orders. I went down to the village square. The car is still there. The tires are deflated, probably because of the heat. I piled straw around them so they wouldn't dissolve into latex. As you know, rubber melts. And of course the houses are still there, but empty. I went in them and there was no one. I wonder what the point of them is. These peasants are crazy to burrow into mountain holes when there are barracks, half-demolished perhaps, but with several walls still standing.

— Where are the suspects? repeated the chief. It was like an echo. Where is Raho? And Hajja? Bourguine?

The inspector immediately put a long distance call through to his head, PCV.* He was on the point of offering some impeccably clear, imponderable rationale, the very same in fact which the Minister of Justice had just recently developed on television when, for a full hour, he had never lost the thread of his blossoming thought in the forest of figures and commas. The Minister "did not necessarily reject amendment 21, article 2, which impinged upon article 7-A of the Bill on criminality, which tended to supercede article 165 of the penal code through provisions of which whereby the keeper of the Great Seal indeed preferred to keep the third, but not the fifth which appeared to him to indicate double usage of article L-267 of the health code, certainly, however . . ." Yes, Inspector Ali, ever respectful of the big shots, was quite ready to throw himself into equally rational explanations; however, he saw his chief's eyes—and in any case, he wasn't on camera. So he said prosaically:

— Thirty-three minus twenty, so there are no more than thirteen left. Yes, chief, yesterday evening, I counted these peasants. Including us, there were thirty-five. There are seven adults and half a dozen children left. With the heat and the weather we're having, I fear that pretty soon we'll be all alone on this mountain with our official mission still hanging over our heads.

— Where are they? asked the chief, who was impressed with his own calm. I'm talking about Hajja, Bourguine and Commander Filagare, not the small fry.

— They're not here. No one who remotely resembles them anywhere. I did hear Raho blow on his old cow horn, but there's no sign of either him or his

*Morocco's Ma Bell

donkey. Maybe they've all gone to look for something to feed us. Hospitality is sacred.

There was a pause. The sun sizzled and two lungs sucked in the hot air, and exhaled it down to the last gasp of anger. Then, without raising his voice louder than a murmur, the chief said:

— I would like to know one thing: what is the difference between an imbecile and you?

Inspector Ali rapidly evaluated the distance which separated him from his superior and answered without hesitation:

— Oh, barely one and a half meters.

He quickly added:

— Which is why the imbecile now asks you: aren't we in a mess?

— What mess? The big shots aren't here? So? They will certainly return this evening, and I will grill them then. In the meantime, go find me one of those who are left over.

— OK, chief. Right away. There's one thing, though, which doesn't quite fit in because I have no references whatsoever. Ever since Central woke me up yesterday at 6 a.m. when I was happily sleeping by my wife's side I've been in the dark about what it's all about. What is the goal of our mission, chief? Precisely?

— State secret, the chief answered. You don't go shouting around State secrets to people like you, you Bulgar.

— Ah, he replied with a large smile. Since you put it that way, I understand. It must be very serious for you to put up with all these trials. Horrible discomfort all around, and not a creature comfort anywhere. Understood, chief. I'm off.

7

— Come on. You, come in, said the inspector to the shadow which followed close behind him. Make yourself at home. Please join us. After intoning some brief courtesies, a kind of human poplar tree entered the cavern. His trunk was almost as high as the top of the tree and was perpendicular to it. He was a gnarled peasant, tall, thin and very serious looking. He had a short black beard and a shaven, blue skull.

— Do like the camel, the inspector ordered him.

— What? asked the other.

— Bend your knees, sit down.

— Ah, fine. *Wakhkha*, OK.

He spat in his hands and rubbed them against each other while saying, "In the name of Allah," and then he sat.

— Stand up! the Chief of Police ordered. What kind of manners do you have?

— What?

— Stand up!

— Ah, fine, said the mountain man. OK.

And, after another invocation to the creator of mountains and of men, he stood back up like a folding yard stick. Upright, his head bent and his shoulders supporting the roof of the cavern, he towered over the chief. He didn't do a thing, didn't say a word. His contemplative regard switched between one policeman and the other like a metronome.

The chief turned his eyes upward 180 degrees and said:

— No, no, that won't do at all. There's something wrong here.

— What?

— Sit down.

— Bend your knees, added the inspector.

— Ah! Fine, said the peasant. *Wakhkha*, OK. Anything is possible with the help of Allah.

He sat down again quietly. During this time, half a dozen children of all ages had appeared at the entrance of the cavern, some dressed in rags, others stark naked. One of them decided to enter, and the others followed him. They all sat down and waited for the show. Despite the chief's furious gestures encouraging them to disperse, they congregated around him, ears straining.

— Go away! Take off! Beat it! he cried. Out! Not one of them budged, nor gave the slightest indication of comprehension. Their eyes were warm, the trusting color of charcoal. The inspector waved his arms about as if he were chasing flies and said:

— Kchch! Kchch! Get a move on. Go play, little ones. Go away! *Go away!*

They retained their innate stoicism. From early childhood to puberty, none of them ever reacted to the sound of words or shouts, except for one sickly urchin who began to scratch his armpit.

— I'm going to get angry, yelled the chief. And if I get angry, it's all over. Enough of this nonsense. Get out!

The mountain man let out a little cough, followed by a remark:

— They love stories. They're kids, after all.

— Are they yours? asked the chief.

— Some are. Those three over there. They are of the blood of my wife and myself. The others are cousins, maybe nephews. They don't make any noise, do they?

— Noise or no noise, tell them to shake a leg. Get out the broom!

— What?

— This is going to be men's talk, explained the inspector. Can you tell them to go away with their childishness?

— Ah, replied the bearded one. (There was a noise like a locomotive releasing steam—his way of laughing, evidently.) Ah! Sir, I ask you, is there no shame left in this world? They know the things of life better than any adult. Yes, ha, ha, oh yes.

— Just the same, tell them to leave.

— Fine. With Allah's permission, OK.

Without looking at them, he addressed the children in a regretful tone.

— Tomorrow, he said to them. No stories today. Tomorrow, *incha Allah*!

Slowly they stood up and went away, without a word, without turning around. It was as though they had never existed.

— Good, said the chief. We can now begin our friendly discussion, get to know each other. Was the harvest good this year?

— Well, sir, Allah did what he could. The prickly pears grew with all their thorns. As you know, they don't need to be watered.

— How about the wheat, the barley, the corn? The other grains?

— Well, sir, the peasant answered, there's nothing to say about it. Such is life.

— So it was a good harvest?

— Sir, you would do best to go back down to the plains and take whatever soul you've got with you. Yes, perhaps that's best.

The chief, who had up to then been as sinuous as a snake, immediately found his viper's tongue and retreated to attack posture. His hand rolled up into a menacing fist which he began to twist upwards like a hammer straightening a bent nail.

— And what in Allah's name do you mean by that?

— I mean what I said, sir, replied the mountain man without elaborating. Allah is with all of us and none of us. No earth, no rain, at least very little, no government seed grain—so, sir, where do you expect to find all the good things in life which you were talking about, except in your empty head? Are you a tourist? You nevertheless look like an Arab like me. Who knows?

The chief, taking the inspector as his witness, said with intense incredulousness:

— But really . . . really, did you hear that?

— My goodness, of course he heard me. I've only got one tongue. Oh, I see he's scribbling down my words with that number 2 pencil of his, but I said what I said.

The man composing the police symphony immediately abandoned the first interrogatory movement and broadjumped over to the finale: a crescendo of decibels which expressed the true state of human relations in this, the end of the 20th century. The dominators, and the dominated, nothing more. The kow-towers had indeed paralyzed the Orient, oh yes.

— Name, first name, on the double!

— What?

— What is your name?

— Oh, sir, no need to shout. My name is your brother's.

— I have no brother. What is your name?

— Well, sir, put yourself in my place, and your answer will be fine. Surely.

— *Ladin Babek!* Curse your father. Do you know who I am? Well? The mountain man smiled for the first time. It was a slow, unmalicious, patient smile.

— Oh, yes, sir, he replied. You are a man who shouts and insults your hosts.

And with the help of his hands laid flat against the ground, he started to rise.

— Where are you going? Stay seated! That's an order.

— Sir, time nourishes life, and my life is on the verge of dying through starvation.

— I . . . I am, the chief screamed, I am . . . a government functionary.

— That's what Hajja told me. Maybe so.

— I am . . . I'm the Chief of Police, the . . . the State's police.

The man on the ground began to laugh, as though at the sight of an unexpected flower growing in the rubble.

— That's what Hajja told me, he repeated. Right now, everyone in the world knows it, even beyond the village. So? There's still no rain.

With no forewarning, the sovereign act annihilated all words, and in a single movement, the chief opened his travel bag, pulled out his revolver and fired without aiming. And with him, the new masters of the Third World, wrapped in their human dignity, also pulled the trigger and fired. "Chief," the inspector cried out. The bullet had nicked his ear, and he continued to yell "Chief!" in every possible tone of voice, from fear to bedside manner. The smoke drifted off, the sounds of the shot died away, and nothing remained but several curious onlookers, women, children, and men collected at the entrance to the grotto. And when they had ascertained that there were no dead, nor any son of Adam writhing in agony, they slowly disappeared, followed by their shadows. As if the flaming sun outside had made all their doubts vanish. There remained the peasant, still seated in all his earnestness, still with his black beard and blue skull. And he said with the voice of destiny:

— Several years ago, the earth shook, yonder, far from here, in a city of the plains and the mountains. It was called Agadir, I believe, according to what the Saharan nomads said . . . And oh, sir, some died, some survived. Different ones. But Allah is great for both.

The revolver had been aimed at the peasant' head from his first words, then at his belly, then at his mouth from which issued outrageous rebellion, now menacing his superior position at his shoulder, behind him, there, at the very lip of the cave, ready to wipe it out, there between his legs, all the descendants to come, humans, animals, "chimpanzee-esque types". All of that hammered on the chief so that his neck vein pulsed to an explosive rhythm, swollen with black blood.

84

— . . . The next time . . . the next time, I won't miss. I'll score, and I have the right, you . . . you filthy hound!

— Ah, fine. O.K. If it is *mektoub*, it's *mektoub*. Everything is written in the sky. Even you.

— *Ladin mouk!* You son of a cursed bitch! You are under arrest. Papers! Right now!

— Ah, sir, said the other without raising his voice, Allah only knows what makes you so full of gas, but don't go spewing all over other people. It's useless and doesn't intimidate anyone.

It was at that instant that the inspector intervened, creating a cease-fire at the very moment his chief was about to kill for real. He had learned his weapons in numerous urban demonstrations and riots, dressed in civvies, and he knew how to wield a club or an iron bar against the forces of order. Nothing easier after that than to organize the ringleaders into cells and set them up for a trap. He knew all the back streets of the *medina*. He had been born and reared there, and had become a man in those streets. He had it all: a slang vocabulary capable of making even a Moroccan's hair curl, a revolting set of clothes, and the look of a beggar. He could sing the *Internationale* in Arabic as well as he could the Palestinian anthem, or the Polisario rally. He was rather pleased when he was bashing his colleagues, not that he took the least pride or what have you in it. He was equally content when they would drag some handcuffed heckler into his office. Same difference. Ah, but what a job it was. What kind of humorless chief was this? He put on his submissive look and, leaping into the two-person riot, he addressed his chief in French:

— He's nothing but trash, chief.

The chief looked at him in a stupor, his mouth open. His breathing rose and fell with the noise of a frog's bellows.

— Worthless small fry, the inspector continued quickly. A rotten sardine—You, you're a big fish, you're a big strapping fellow in comparison. See? Sacred to the State.

And without waiting for a response, he turned to the peasant, and once facing him, changed his face into its *"aspect populaire"*, *sui generis*, lowest social classification, third-class railway expression. In his meanest market bargaining voice, he began to berate the peasant:

— Listen, you *Untel*, you with your head scalped, and Allah always in your mouth! Well, cram your foot in your mouth and stuff it for a while. My chief over there is a very important man, so important that jerks like you sometimes have to wait three to six months and more just to get into his office for the privilege of his glancing at their files! Do you got cow shit stuffed in your ears, and everywhere else for that matter?

The mountain man listened to this outburst and looked at him, trying to interpret the winks he was receiving, the set of his mouth, the charade his nervous face was playing out for him. And as he began to understand, his smile grew broader. He said:

— You I understand. I understand you perfectly. You're talking like an Arab. Politely.

— So shut up and listen to what I'm telling you. Right? There you have a man who is both government and police and who's taken the trouble to climb up all the way to your little hole and this is how you receive him? If I didn't intervene on your behalf, you'd be in dutch forever. That's what you deserve, all of you. Nothing but a bunch of bean heads! And to think that the chief came here to help you! . . . Go on, spit on the ground!

— You know our customs, don't you? said the peasant.

And he spat. The inspector also deposited a wad on the floor before turning round to face his chief with a conspiratorial expression.

— Should I nick that rotten sardine, chief? Then you go after the whales with your harpoon? How about it, chief?

Exhausted by the fury which had run its course, his back covered with sweat and his tongue dry, the chief nodded, twice.

— OK, chief. I'm going to knock the wind out of this guy. You'll see the works.

Well then! What kind of person was this police chief? Propelled towards the top, the day after Independence, because he had been heaving sand and lime into ditches, and most of the time, digging other holes, what in fact could this man know? He could only be overwhelmed by the dramatic sense of his own importance. Like all the other chiefs in countless different administrations, for years he couldn't get over the fact that he occupied such a high position, and wielded real power, in the form of the law and its execution. Elsewhere, in other offices, there were the same types, all chiefs: religious types promoted to magistrates, just because they knew by heart, or almost, two or three chapters of the Koran; Montebanks and hagiographers lording over the destinies of broadcasting, television, the arts, and religious schools, the Council of Distinguished Authors; secretary generals, directors, offices, documents, records. A plethora of chiefs formed one big giant iron tree, rigid in both directions: horizontal and vertical. "Stamp out those thoughts," the inspector said to himself angrily. "One of these days, you'll say them out loud and then watch out . . . And what good will it do, anyway? What are you, anyway, but a treadmill? Dominator and dominated at the same time, the perfect spot, what! . . . like a finger between the nail and the hammer. You get knocked on the head, and you knock the guy below you . . . that's the police. That's your work, you poor little inspector. Come on, stop thinking. Now. The chief is looking at you.

— Were you speaking to him in *roumi*?* asked the peasant, pointing at the chief with his thumb.

— Yes, I was talking to him in Frankish, so what's it to you? He and I, we understand each other that way. It's official. It's like the right and the left hands. Got it?

— No.

— Doesn't matter. Let's move on, my brother. The chief asked for your papers. Do you have any papers?

*Roman, lit., French or Frankish

86

— There used to be once upon a time, the mountain man replied. Hajja used them to light the fire one day. Old boxes.

— That's not it, said the inspector patiently. You see, in the city people have all kinds of papers stuffed in their pockets.

— We're not in the city, my friend.

— I'll explain it to you. Give me your hand, old man. They have both papers and cards. Do you understand?

— No, said the peasant. I haven't the faintest idea what you're talking about.

— Let me explain again to you, repeated the inspector tenaciously. There are pink ones, and blue ones, ones of every color. There are some you need to drive a car, two in fact: a gray card to have the car, and a pink one to put it on the road. It's simple.

— Well, after all, I don't have a car. Just a mule and a donkey over there. See for yourself. And if you think a piece of paper will get them to move, you must be joking!

— Patience, my brother, the inspector urged, mopping his brow. Fine, you don't have a permit, you don't have a car, I can't do anything about it. But they have them in the cities. Round and round. You should see it! Let's go on to something else. Come closer. Listen.

— Fine, OK.

— There are other papers, loads of them. A voter registration card, for example?

— What are you talking about? I don't understand Frankish.

— OK, you don't vote either. Let's leave that. Boy, are we going to have a hot day!

— No hotter than yesterday. It's summer. In winter it's less hot.

— Yes. Fine. Well, let's skip over the Social Security part, and the Family Assistance Allocation because insofar as you are the head of a family, you nevertheless get nothing from the government, right?

— I don't know anyone in the government. On the other hand, there are two guys whom I wouldn't know from Adam, who come once a year to take away our animals as a tax.

— I know, I know, the inspector replied immediately to reassure him. Don't get angry. That's ancient history. In any case, they won't come again since you have nothing to give them. But tell me, there's also the Family Registration Record. You're married, aren't you?

The peasant gave him a pitying smile, exposing his gums.

— You should tread carefully and watch what you say. Do you suppose I could have produced those three kids you saw earlier all by myself?

— You're right, said the inspector. I forgot. Women are necessary in such situations. They do their duty and provide you pleasure. It has to be. Congratulations, my brother! I wish you happiness and plenty! And five or six more. You're in the prime of your years as far as I can see. So it's written down somewhere that you're married, isn't it? In some notary public's little black book . . . in a Family Registration Record, as we say in this modern administration?

— Oh, no sir, no, the mountain man replied. We're in the country here. Nothing's been scribbled down. No one knows how to scribble around here in any case. We very properly recited a little chapter from the Koran after having washed our faces and hands—that's the way the custom goes. We sang, danced and then ate. And then, before entering my tent (I had a tent in those days), I said to my wife: "Zohra, daughter of the Beni Mellil, I take you as my wife. I swear it." I gave her my word, do you understand? She gave me hers as well. She said to me, eyes lowered, "Ali, son of the Ait Yafelman, you will be my husband. I also swear it."

— By Allah and the Prophet, the inspector cried out, his eyes suddenly alight. You're called "Ali", just like me!

He embraced him and congratulated him warmly, slapping him on the back, and calling him dear cousin. With a kind of gaiety, he turned around to the chief.

— Chief, his name is Ali, just like mine. It's amazing.

But, by Allah, he thought, that wild one has lost his senses. What kind of a chief is he? Killing people *before* the interrogation, ha! Yes, indeed, . . . and then later, giving himself meningitis in his office, typing away with his two index fingers on that stupid old *makina tomatik*, pages upon pages about what the corpse volunteered before going bananas and assaulting a police officer who was merely doing his duty. For that was the hardest, most inhuman part of the profession: writing, inventing, pushing one's imagination across the steppes of words, and the Sahara of ideas. Certainly, certainly! There was some recompense for this fantastic intellectual excursion. The work having been finished at breakneck speed, there was the satisfaction of holding in one's hands the prescribed 21 x 29.7 manuscript, sheets correctly typed single space, lining it up on the desk and tapping it down with little hammer-like blows on the top and the sides. (Until just recently, one was supposed to type double space with a wide margin, to let it "breathe": so the regulations specified. And then came the paperwork explosion in the police department. No more need, consequently, for so much wasted space between two lines, staring you in the face . . . What's more, wasn't there a note posted in all departments proclaiming the government's new policy of austerity?)

— He's Ali, chief, he repeated. Give him a little friendly spot in your assistance program for underdeveloped peasants. He's called Ali, chief. He at least deserves a little *bakchich*.

The chief didn't deign to glance at him. He placed his revolver nearby in case he became enraged again and, with a stony face, he reread the notes he had just taken, his mechanical pencil tracing over the words line by line, his lips moving silently. Without raising his head, he finally said:

— Speak more slowly.

— What?

— You're going too fast, I can hardly follow you.

— OK, chief. I'll slow down the gears. And you, he said to the mountain man, go gently at an even pace. We've got the whole day ahead of us. There's no hurry.

The son of the soil stared for a good, long moment. His mouth opened to express a certain incredulity.

— Just like that, my countryman? That man starts off by shooting at me, and now hear him talk about giving me money. It used to be that if you sowed wheat, you harvested wheat. Hey, don't give me that look, my fellow.

— He wasn't shooting at you! Don't believe that, brother. Ali, think about it. Ali! He was simply loosening up his fingers. It's the same every morning. He must make sure that his weapon is working. Understand?

— No. It's inexplicable.

— See here, you're confusing different things in your head. You're mixing them up: primo, the chief's hand has to get warmed up. After a night of sleep, it gets rusty. And this pistol has to shoot properly every single one of Allah's days. Secondly, you exchanged words with the chief, and his anger mounted, just as bread rises, and so just see how coincidences work: it was just at that moment that the chief thought to try out his weapon. Don't go confusing the head of a dog with his tail. You're an adult with three children who, Allah willing, will grow up to be adults themselves.

— Ah, said the peasant, one eye closed, the other wide open. Fine. Since you put it like that. Perhaps he regrets his action?

— Him? Regret? You donkey head, there's nothing to regret. I tell you, my brother, I tell you he would have fired in any event, even if you hadn't been there.

— But I was there.

— It's the same as if you weren't. It's that simple. Forget it.

— Oh? Alright. And you say you're going to give me some money?

— If it turns out that way. Hmm, yes, if it comes about.

— So let's have it now, and may Allah bless him this very moment. It's not worth talking about any further. Tell him that there have been whole moons and seasons when I haven't seen a piece of copper or nickel. Speak to him in Frankish, he'll understand more quickly.

And he held out his hands.

— No, no, the inspector said quickly. There again, you're thinking like a peasant. If I were passing out the manna, there'd be no problem, by Allah and the prophet, and the Prince of Believers who governs over us from one of his palaces, from one of his thrones because, no doubt, he has a throne in every palace. Say Amen!

— Amen! said the peasant.

— No, it's not me, the inspector continued. I'm going to get through that old piece of leather you've got wrapped around your brain and get you to understand how the administration works. Do you know what the administration is?

— No.

— Doesn't matter. Imagine a huge house in the city, full of well-dressed people who are well-fed, and who live surrounded by mountains of paper. They've got to have papers. And you don't have any. Therefore you don't exist for them. That's the story. You haven't been born, you're not alive, and you're not even dead. Very sad, wouldn't you say? What are we going to do about it? Do you have a notion, or even the glimmer of an idea?

— No, answered the peasant, bug-eyed.

— Me neither.

— So don't go on about this fortune, concluded the peasant. That's for the rich people, not for us. There are some kettles which are always bubbling over, and there are others which are always empty. That's the way it is. May you have a peaceful day, my brother. I'm going to take off.

— Stay here, said the inspector. Save your wife for this evening. You've got time. You're always *zouc-zoucing* her. Let her rest a little! If I were to tell you I haven't had any nooky for 36 hours through circumstances beyond my control . . .

— You're wandering, Inspector Ali!

— What?

— You're vulgar. And what's more, you're straying from the path.

— Oh, no, chief, don't think that, the inspector protested. All roads lead to prison and besides, I know the shortcuts.

— Enough!

— But chief, it's just one way to reach our goals. There are expressways, and there are mule paths. When the questions become too abstract, when they get a little slack, if you know what I mean, well, what's the harm in spicing them up a bit? Harden things up a bit, what?

— I said: Enough.

— Yes, chief, that's what you said. I certainly heard it. But I know our peasants. I'm like them. When I get excited, if you catch my drift, my tongue loosens up. Who knows why. Human nature, probably. The only thing that fellow there can still do freely in our country, is the *bagatelle*. *Zouc-zouc*. A little wham-bam. Isn't that right, my brother?

— Ah, fine, the peasant answered with a wide smile. You know the human soul, don't you?

— Somewhat. A little bit. It helps you to get through life. If there weren't you know what, oh cousin! I wonder how there'd be any commerce. There are some people who emigrate for nothing but . . .

— Enough! the chief screamed, his face the color of his spleen. Get him out of here!

— But, chief, the interrogation hasn't even really begun. I was just on the access road, atomic love,* as the poets who write poems say. In a moment, the curtain's going to rise, and the rabbit's going to pop out of the hat.

— Unload this vermin right away . . . immediately, almighty Allah . . . if you don't I swear by the Turks and the Greeks that I'll . . . I'll . . . out!

— Did you hear him? He said, 'out!' the inspector informed the mountain man with great severity. So out! *Fissa!* Do like the camel after a wonderful

---

*I believe the inspector wanted to say "platonic love," but I couldn't be sure. —*Note from author.*

90

siesta, unfold your legs and move on. Out of here! You undocumented male! Move on before two and two no longer make four. Go on, find your worthy wife. Giddiup!

The peasant studied the two policemen, one after the other. Then he slowly got up and went away, like a tall sapling, chanting under the sun some invocation to the one who created the simple-minded and the lunatics.

As of that moment, the chief began seriously to ponder this god-forsaken investigation—and the meaning of life in general, in case it should prove useful. For two hours, he sat there, taking stock of the situation, doing inventory mentally on his fingers, eyes closed, struggling mightily against sleep, and also against the fire and blood of consciousness. During these two hours, Inspector Ali spoke to him three times, at spaced intervals. This is what he said:

1) If I only knew what we were investigating in this backwater.
2) Fine. I think I'll take a little stroll to pass the time.
3) Are you sleeping, chief?

The Chief of Police didn't glance at him, lost as he was among the jumble of his thoughts which he had to reassemble like so many ruins, stack up and stick together with the only cement available to him, his willpower.

Between the second and third remarks, the inspector had had plenty of time to go down into the village to strike up a conversation with someone, anyone, anything with four limbs, two ears and a tongue! He missed human intercourse. He didn't much like drama, and as best he knew, there wasn't the slightest trace of humor in funerals, whether in the city or in the country. He vaguely remembered a certain "Racine son of Athalie" from his school days, with serpents hissing around his head in the days when he took up a whole school bench near the door. But that was the past, and thanks to Allah, most merciful and benificent, and thanks too to the police, he was done with sharpening pencils. That was the truth! He had been sick of it. There were limits to everything, even in a police station. The inspector would conduct his own investigation, and he'd see what he would see! Let the chief keep all the elements at his disposal, the why and the wherefore, the centrifugal sense! Let him implode, that egotist. He and his ilk, the big chiefs in all the bureaucracies and even in the soccer leagues, all had a single policy: to keep everything for themselves: to keep chewing away on their own little "chiefdoms". Inspectors like himself, staff personnel, assistants—not even to mention the bottom rungs of the ladder!—should and could do nothing but fill up the gas tanks, lace up the chief's boots, listen to them, approve of them, admire them and carry their bags. The French had gone, but their slaves stayed behind— porters, domestics, intermediaries jammed for good between the new masters of the Third World and the people. Oh, by Allah and the Prophet, he'd conduct his own investigation under the scorching sun, if only to get to know the villagers a bit. For the last thirty-six hours they'd been in this place, they hadn't been able to glean the smallest piece of information on their lives, their desires, and their needs. It wasn't even a matter of simple police-like curiosity, but rather merely an effort to get to know the mood of the country. And right now, what did they know about these mountain people? Two times zero equals zero, plus a few scrapings and scraps. What kind of work was this: ask questions, get answers, noting them down at the same time in an old pocket pad with a gold mechanical pencil? To what end this pencil policy? A stupid little coincidence in a hay stack: a peasant whose first name was Ali, like him. Ha! Hoho, haha! At this speed, he'd need at least two or three years to bring this official mission—about which he hadn't the slightest clue—to an end.

By *Allah Akbar*, as Khomeini says, the only kind of useful investigation here is an oral one, as in oral culture of the countryside, as in the good old *zouc-zouc*. My goodness, you don't go up to these people with a notebook in hand! Lucky the chief didn't think, in his paranoia, to cart along a typewriter. The inspector grinned like a mountain ass at the thought of setting up the latest model *machineautomatik* on a hillside stone and saying to a son of the soil: "Be patient, oh countryman! Hold on while I put these two pieces of paper and a carbon into the roller. Go ahead. I'm listening. And be brief. I don't have much paper."

He burst right out laughing, and then he saw Hajja. What great luck! There she was, apparently unoccupied, within earshot of the cavern, as though she were expecting some conversation. He greeted her respectfully, kissed her hands in the ancient anti-oedipal tradition, and addressed her as "Little Mother" and "Mamma". He was so happy to see her! For a second, he thought of discipline and duty—he ought to drag Hajja over to his superior since she was one of the big shots. It would have been so easy to nab her by only taking her hand if she had shown the least resistance to his request. But maybe the dough had not had enough time to rise, and above all, he mustn't disturb Chief Mohammed in his cerebral enterprise. He finally fished up a little idea, or to say the least, he grabbed the devil by the tail. Yes, stones could bear fruit if you only had the patience to wait. Haven't they been saying since the Crusades, at least the French had been, that the quintessential Arab virtue was patience? They even called it fatalism. Inspector Ali was born of Arabs who were born of Arabs, not one of these grade B American T.V. series detectives!

— Let's see. now" he said to himself, "it's not my investigation. I don't even know what it's about. I don't care royally or administratively! All that matters to me is to stand here, arms crossed, stuff myself, and try to slip between the rain drops. When the chief buys the farm, well, if that happens, I'll take this investigation in hand and carry it out in my own way. Until then, I'm doing nothing. I'm a true Arab. Let the chief muddle through with his cogitations and his revolver! I'd be real happy if he'd just put a bullet in his brain, oh, yes indeed!

Oddly, Hajja's eyes had a different look in them from the night before, even from this morning when he had discussed the matter of the uniform buttons with her. It seemed to him she avoided his gaze. Probably because the sun was directly in her eyes. That must be the explanation, as surely as three plus four make . . . she didn't even want to chat. She left him in the middle of a greeting which was as long as a boa which hadn't fully uncoiled. And she took off, without even saying good-bye, or see you later at lunch. Her bare feet pattered quickly and with agility against the ground before her. All around her the fine dust rose, and then slowly settled.

— Phooey! he said to himself. She's wracking her brains, no doubt, trying to figure out how to use last night's old bones. She could have talked to me about it, all the same! I would have given her some recipes my mother used to make. Sometimes, she'd fix up in the oven some wonderful little dishes with nothing but scraps. Those were the good old days!

He let out a long sigh, pulled up his hood so he wouldn't get sun stroke, and started to go down the torturous little path which led to the village square. The chief surely wouldn't croak over it. And anyway, weren't his thoughts kind of slow? "Ali, what did you say to him? Think back, word for word. You said to him, 'I think I'll take a walk', or rather, 'a *little* walk' ." The inspector's memory was heated up, and, under the flaming dome of the sky, would soon slowly consume itself. As if he had never had any memories at all.

— The chief will understand, he concluded out loud. He's got the head for it. A walk is a walk, whether a small one or a long one. It's all the same.

Raho was in the process of wielding his pick, trying to scrape a hole in soil as unyielding as civilization. Patiently, without hurrying, without a single drop of sweat on his forehead. How could he not be soaking wet? He grasped the tool with both hands, raised it above his head, and chanted "Allah!" the way others grunted "Huhnh, huhnh!" in those lands without religious tradition. "Allah!" Each time he struck, the point of the pick bit the earth and gave off with each blow two or three sparks and some chunks of dirt.

The inspector stopped, watched him work for a long moment, and said:

— You need a jackhammer, grandfather. One of those machines that go *bzzzzzrrr-bzzzzrrriiikkk*, breaking up sidewalks and bursting ear drums. There are some modern road gangs who use them in the city, especially during summer, the *Amirikanes* tourist season. That way the *Amirikanes* know that we're using their equipment, and that we, the other half, work hard. That Arabs aren't a bit like those Indians with feathers, or those turbaned types from *Ali Voud*. Oh, I used to laugh when I'd see those films! Can you believe our brothers in the movie business could be so rich and have such confusing tongues! And gibbering away they go in one of those crazy languages that even I can't get the sense of, even the tiniest bit. Those guys I was telling you about, their arms don't stop shaking even at night. Obviously, it's those jackhammers. It seems that their wives sleep separately, since the conjugal bed doesn't stop bouncing around. They're former peasants who came down from their mountains so they could earn something to buy a T.V. and walk their families around the supermarket at the end of the week. But I bet you don't even know what a T.V. is, right?

— Aha! replied Raho, dismissing this barrage of words with a semi-circle sweep of his pick-axe.

— Yes, indeed, continued the inspector, his mouth full of saliva. I had a friendly chat with one of those guys in the course of asking him for his identity papers, work papers, and all that. And to make sure they were enrolled with the right unions. Do you know what a Union is, hunh? Well, you're right, Uncle. And then when there's an official funeral, you got quickly to clear up places, make sure there're no work gangs and bums. You got to camouflage the holes quick, *fissa*, sometimes with canvas, often with flags. The Service truck is always nearby, right ahead of the T.V. truck. You gotta to do what you gotta do, right? You don't know the city, pops, so let me lay it out for you. You don't have to look too far behind the words to see the meaning. A nice hard dirt street is quite pretty, and besides, it saves you on paving stones. You don't see these things in the Christian or pagan countries. Believe it or not, grand-dad, but these country boys don't even remember what a simple plow looks like! Is this good or bad? I don't know. I never get mixed up with politics. But you don't know what politics is, do you? These fellows become amnesiac and I wonder how long they've been that way. On the other hand, they'll talk to you about choppers jerry-rigged from all kinds of used parts, not like a Japanese machine from Japan . . . about motorbikes with handlebars as familiar to the grip as the bridles of a horse in the old days. Well, my chief's up there . . . let's not go on about it any more. Do you think you'll succeed with your little pickaxe in this rock, under the devil's own sun?

— I don't know, said Raho. I must dig.

— Yes, quite true. Most certainly. If you don't dig, you won't have a hole. Not the least bit of a hole. Are you going to plant a date-palm?

— Oh, no. No, I'm just digging a hole.

Raho looked him squarely in the eye and said very simply:

— A grave.

— A grave? By Allah and the Prophet, did someone die in the village while I was sleeping peacefully away?

— Oh no, not yet.

— What do you mean by that?

— Man is born, lives his life, then dies, the mountain man explained.

— So who dies? Who's going to die?

Raho slowly s⁺ ʾdied the horizon in the east, then in the west; he studied the sky where human destiny is inscribed, and the earth on which he stood. Then he held out three fingers, and folded them one by one as he gently replied:

— I don't know much. Maybe one man. Maybe two. Perhaps a third. Only Allah knows.

— Yes, obviously, said the inspector, who was experiencing an abrupt heat flash. Clearly. You are old, and you see your next home . . . He talked on for a good ten minutes, on the pure air of the mountains, the wholesome food, the absence of electric guitars, punk rock; the sturdy bones of the peasants made up of natural calcium, of this and of that. He didn't get a single word of approval, or even a glance of interest. He ended up by washing his hands of it, or more precisely, he left Raho in the august hands of Allah who alone knew the right answer. He finally said in the conversational tone of two old friends:

— You haven't by chance seen a gun hanging around here?

The old mountain man allowed himself to put down his pickaxe and asked as if flabbergasted:

— A gun?

— Yes, Inspector Ali joked. A thing with a stock and a barrel, you know. The stock is made of wood and the barrel of metal. It's called a gun.

— A gun, Raho repeated like an echo.

— Yes, that's it. It shoots. It does harm. It takes away the life which Allah gives. You wouldn't have put it away somewhere in the shade safely, so it wouldn't rust up, or so some kid, quite innocently to be sure, just fooling around, no doubt, doesn't go shooting at government grown-ups, police, like they do sometimes in the city?

— Aha! Is that the way they amuse themselves in the city?

— It happens. It happens, said the inspector. And you're obliged to lock them up before they've even started high school. They don't know what they're doing. They start off with our local hashish, *Kif*, and then go on from there: kung fu, their fix, and their speed. Their parents watch T.V. They barely have enough to eat, but they have their sacred T.V. So they obviously don't have the time to give their brats a few feudal beatings which helped you and me to get through life, me in the government, you on your mountain. So Commander, you who know the value of a hard smack and a weapon, did you put the old blunderbuss out of reach of parricides? Is that it?

Raho seemed to think about it. He looked at his pick, at the inspector's face, the slot in the earth which was beginning to take shape at his feet. Then he said, with a note of sadness:

— The partridge gun?

— Yes, indeed! the inspector exclaimed joyfully. Where could I find it right now?

— Over there.

— Where, there?

— There.

— But where? Point out the general location to me.

— It's far, said Raho. I'll give it to you this evening. There's time enough.

— Why not now?

— The grave isn't finished yet. There's the whole afternoon ahead of us.

— But you'll give it to me this evening? Promise? By Allah and the Prophet?

Raho looked at him for a long time, his face completely lined with wrinkles, and it was as though he were making a tremendous effort to hold back his tears. Then he sniffed, and with great good will flowing from his voice and his eyes, he said:

— Yesterday, you asked me for the hospitality of Allah. Therefore, you can trust my word. It hasn't changed.

And that was all. The pickaxe rose up with the heavy weight of destiny and rang out against the rock, shattering the mystery of death in bursts of stone and thought. Despite an abbreviated but affable interrogation marked by almond paste and honey, and which from the very prolegomena leaped immediately from the track of dry, rational facts into the esoteric morass of the great, universal themes, such as 'the unreality of the earth and the skies, and of all between the two' or 'the paradise and hell which are naught but the playthings of children, you see, Raho, what must be done must be done, grand-dad, religion has got to take another quarter turn, don't you know!' . . . Ali nevertheless couldn't drag a single word from the old man, no complementary information about the grave which he was making deeper and deeper, nor even about the approximate identity of the one who was to die, not a single warning down at the precinct, no cooperation—nothing but the punctuating blows of iron biting the ground. Torn from mother earth, the stones spun off into the air like so many replies to the single, metallic syllable.

When he realized that the pebbles and rocks were starting to pile up around his ankles, he decided to take off. Reluctantly, as he was in the middle of a sonorous sentence examining the predicament of man cornered between two mirages: death, which pushed from behind, and life's ever-receding horizon. He wondered how on earth during his police career he could have ever dug up this awfully sinister soliloquy, rhymed and rhythmed like a Koranic verse—and whose meaning he didn't even quite understand, even as he translated it into the simple concreteness of Moroccan dialect. Feeling sad and abandoned, he began to clamber up the mountain trail. And as he rose higher toward the cavern, and duty, he ran through his mind the raw actuarial tables. By Allah and the Prophet, he would never know by what mental process he had been able to move so quickly from spiritualism to materialism. For one moment, while he was brilliantly exercising his gray matter, trying to extract a coherent thought in this excruciating heat, he had a kind of sudden premonition: a shadow was following him, menacing, yet at the same time warning him of imminent danger. For just an instant, he felt his skin crawl.

The man who experienced this signal was no longer the seasoned and crafty policeman who was masked in the guise of simplicity, but the old street-wise tramp who had, through necessity, in his adolescence, been a petty thief, a scrounger, a pickpocket capable of identifying an undercover cop in a crowd, or a bulging wallet in a line outside the movie theater nestled in the pocket of some smug bourgeois. With the agility of a chimpanzee, in one smooth movement, he quickly crouched down and leaped around, holding a rock with each hand. His breath was shallow, his lips curled back.

He saw nothing but his own shadow, still as he, and on the alert, projecting onto the earth his two arched legs and his arms fixed in a position of close combat. And all around him, as far as his eye could see, from the crests of the mountains to the high flats of the western plateaux, everything was biblically calm. The sun was still in the sky, the silence its usual white noise, and way down, old Raho seemed to smile at him benevolently, standing up next to the grave, his hands crossed on the handle of the pickaxe, chin resting on his fist. Did he really look like a sparrow hawk, sharp and direct as a black arrow, ready to leap across the distance separating them, and land straight and true between the inspector's own two eyes? Or was it merely an optical illusion?

— Now listen here, said Inspector Ali to himself, dropping his two stones, one after the other. I'm suffering only from the Third World Hunger Concerto. Next time I go on a mission, I certainly won't trust the chief. I'll arm myself with a diplomatic pouch, a bag overflowing with *hargma** and *mhencha***. I swear it, that's what I'll do to make sure I can see straight. Besides, of all the succulent foods of my country, that's what I like best. I remember my mother, Allah rest her soul, used to get up early to make *hargma*. She . . ."

Right near him, a glance away, a peasant was seated between two bushes withered by three or four months of sun, and his thin fingers roamed up and down the length of a long desert flute. But he didn't sound a single note. Inspector Ali would've loved to play with him one of those traditional airs that you could dance to, clapping, but which you almost never found on the juke boxes. At the very least, he would've liked to start up a conversation about grasshoppers, or even politics. But the mountain man had his eyes closed, and his mouth was open to the July sun—maybe he was doing some little calculations, wouldn't you know.

Two young laughing women were walking side by side with the same swaying step, each one carrying a drum on a sling around her neck. Their buttocks were perfect half moons, their breasts like pointed cones. And by Allah and the Prophet, each was the color of cinnamon which is what Ali really loved. By Beelzebub and all the demons of human heat! Walking across his path, their eyes became liquid, and they took their time staring at him, like women and like children at the same time, part way between candor and desire, between amber and ginger. Their lips were slightly parted and their tongues, pink and firm as country clits, slowly moistened their mouths

---

*hargma, a popular "heavy" dish of sheep's foot and chick peas, spiced—and what spices!
**mhencha, a king's dessert, the preparation of which for an entire harem, takes easily three days.

97

from one side to the other. That was all they did. Not a single word. Happy to look at him with their ever more melting eyes. Happy to promenade the little tips of their quivering tongues, like palpitating incarnations of desire.

— Allah is great! murmured the inspector. *Allah akbar*! he repeated out loud. Allah, come quick to my aid! Lead me not into temptation. By the heat of hell, and besides, I'm in the middle of an investigation for this cursed government. Merciful Allah . . .

Despite his Koranic invocations which uplifted his soul to a state of grace, his earthly envelope was definitely in a state of temptation, beautiful, animal, and—more. With pants made in Singapore, or even Oxford street (London, G.B.), the thing would have clearly been much too visible. And without a doubt, somewhat constrained. But, thanks be to the name of Allah he was wearing a *gandoura*, a rather ample garment. So, simply a fold of cloth had suddenly gently risen up, with no pride whatsoever, shall we say, to the level of his center of gravity, and it swung heavily up and down. I know what I'm saying: Inspector Ali's heart was way overheated—galloping inflation. With his eyes bulging, he cried out immediately:

— Both of you, my little gazelles! I'll marry both of you right now, by Allah and the Prophet! Oh gazelles of matching eyes, breasts and butts, I've never seen anything so beautiful in any precinct of our big beautiful country. This is what I'm going to do . . .

Backing up, they then pressed on, moving off lightly and cheerfully. Their pearly, spiced laughter, trailed behind them in a delightful wake for a long while. Utterly disconsolate, the inspector stood rock still for a moment, completely immobile, breathing heavily through his nose. And then with no warning, he began to cuss out someone to whom he had been extremely attached since his birth:

— Vulgar Arab! he shrieked. Boor! There you stand with an absolute hard-on, I say! Down! Down! You think, you really think, you blue collar pecker, that you're going to lead me around by the nose right up to the bitter end? *Ya wili wili!* Oh! Misery of miseries and of all civilization! Down, I tell you!

Let me specify: His eyes were directed to the middle of his *gandoura*, and he was simply insulting his belt, instructing it to calm down. With two hands, he lowered the thing, twisted it and yelled:

— *Ouille! Ouilouille!* by Allah and the Prophet, what am I going to do now?

. . . .

. . . Somewhat calmed, and more lost than ever, ten minutes later, he started up the path again which led to the grotto, the official repository of the chief, and his duty. His legs were bowed, and he dragged his feet. It was very simple; for him, the investigation was finished. Centuries had been consummated. He was going to hand in his resignation in good and proper form, in other words, orally, in an hour or two, maybe a day or two, in a week at the most—what was time when held up to reality? You could compress it, follow it with a precision watch for sure. You could even stretch it out. He'd end up cornering the chief, face to face, between the little hand which told the hour, and the big one which moved around at its own hasty speed. And he'd talk to him man to man. Ali and Mohammed. A free discussion between two free Arabs. As easy as seven and eight make . . .

No! Oh, no! That wasn't the right method. Your ideas haven't yet had time to breathe a bit, Ali, you onion head! They're still murky. That's what it means to give way to your primordial instincts! No, no! A hundred times no, Inspector Ali, the chief will never listen to you as an equal. He's the *chief*, get it? He's up there, way up there in the administration. He'd never consent to come down off his peak. Rather, tell him . . . : Take your little simple-minded self, your peasant boy, low-grade demeanor and treat your chief like a *chief*: he's a father to you just as the State itself plays the role of *pater familias* to the very nation.

The inspector burst out laughing. And then he began to speak to himself:

— Papa! Papa-chief! Daddy-chief! in the name of most merciful and benificent Allah, master of all worlds, king of the last judgment, place your chiefly hand upon my proletarian pate and bestow upon me your benediction. Father, most respectfully, I implore you for the hand in marriage of those two cinnammon-colored gazelles. Please say yes. I can't go on any longer this way so alone, so solitary. Merely thinking of these two temptresses I lose all joy in life. I'll end up all peevish and scabrous. My glands will swell and burst! So tell me yes right now, oh venerable father. Here the air is not yet polluted, the food is great, in fact it's excellent. I repudiate my old lady— after all you were the first to tell me she was no good. I'll set myself down here for the rest of my days. And since you are the chief, I beg you to be so kind as to accept my most humble resignation and please be assured of my most heartfelt respectful sentiments. Indeed! Despite the enormous efforts that you have continually exerted on my behalf in an attempt to hoist me up to your lofty plateau, I am nevertheless nothing but a simple native. When you return among us to this aboriginal mountain, one day, Allah willing, I'll make you a nice big plate of *hargma* . . . or *hhlii*, that wonderful sun-dried beef which you know so well. Which would you prefer, chief? And anyway, why did you get me into this stupid police force? . . .

He relived those happy days when he used to play soccer. They'd ask him: "So, Ali, who's winning?" "Hey," he'd answer with his big teeth flashing, "we are." And he would add shamelessly, "Thanks to me, king of the turf." As he had neither a PR budget, nor any sort of subsidy, he had been obliged to toot his own horn: with a piece of charcoal he'd scrawl on the walls around town, "Ali, king of the turf." The turf in question was in fact somewhat vague, with no bleachers, surrounded rather by a kind of a ring of his buddies. They weren't, mind you, shoulder to shoulder, but spread out every five or six meters in a kind of ill-defined quadrangle of fluid corners. You think they kept watch all at once on the game, on the two referees and all the gate-crashers? "Hey you over there! Where are you heading to with your pack of peanuts? D'jya pay? Lemme see. You didn't pay! You don't have a stamp on your hand! Beat it! *Fissa!...*"

He saw the police chief's head and he instantly forgot all his resolutions. They were nevertheless irrevocable—the true expression of his real instincts, his real desires. He cleared his throat:

— Hmmhmmmmm!

He cleared his throat and said in a tinny voice:

— Are you asleep, chief?

8

No, the chief was not sleeping. Hardly. If he had closed his eyes it was only because of the blinding light, and he needed to concentrate on his thinking. And if he had done his human best to fend off a sneaked siesta, it was only to his credit. Well-bred people recognize such subtle distinctions. To think, to cogitate cleanly, strongly, to shield the spirit of initiative against the winds and the tides, against the primeval countryside, this infernal heat—this was his lot. No, a hundred times no. The chief had not completely let himself doze off. I can testify to it. You know me. I am a serious man.

During the absence of his subordinate, which he hadn't even been aware of, he had tried to pull everything together. In other words, to evolve, no matter what . . . If this evolution had taken a few zigzags here and there, perhaps a big step forward followed by two or three back, followed in turn by a pro- digious leap into the future bypassing the rest stops of his highway of thought, the result in any case of his sweaty intellectual efforts was this: in the name of all the top-dog police chiefs the world over, including even those of the Orient, this investigation simply could not continue in this manner. There was something that didn't fit, something which clashed. What kind of sand was thrown into the gearbox of the beautifully-designed administrative machinery which heretofore had been so well oiled by the law? Up to now it had always gone without a hitch, damn it! Everyone knew that the law inspired fear, that indeed was its function, its *sine qua non*. Was it possible that the investigation was stalled merely because of uncooperative peasants who hadn't the slightest veneer of civilization? But heavens! . . . if they hadn't the tincture of civilization then that must mean that they were impervious to law and to . . . to fear? Was that then the *corpus delicti*?

— Strange, said the chief to himself. In truth, very strange. In his mind he outlined with a red pencil a very well-defined line of interrogation which he then tucked away into a corner of his vast brain for whatever purpose it could serve in the future. Then, with no further delay, he immediately moved on to the next chapter. He went down deep inside himself. He didn't need pitons or a climbing rope. He knew his own dossier, his *curriculum vitae* as his B.C. Roman colleagues would say.

Oh, but it was exhilarating, by Allah!—and poignant—to follow the trajectory of one man's destiny! Especially if that man was a real-life chief, and if his destiny, solitary to be sure, but nevertheless concentrated as a can of tomato paste, corresponded line by line, decade after decade, to the economic and cultural growth tables of a whole nation. Rising prices and evolving minds? "Perfect," he muttered approvingly. "Excellent." The unemployment figures? "Not me," he said to himself, "not in the police. We even have to drag in recruits. Well, what about the foreign exchange deficit?" The chief laughed!

His eyelids were still closed and even as he sponged the sweat off his brow he began to gently, sweetly shake on the old crate which was his seat, rocked by an unutterable, inner mirth. At a certain moment he started spluttering (triggered by some uncontrollable stimuli), so great had his gaiety become.

— Ha ha! Hahaheeheehouha!—Arf! Arf! . . .

What a sweet joke! For if the balance-of-payments deficit had reached dizzying heights, what was it to him? It wasn't within his sector. It was another sector, that of the pen-pushers. A whole other agency, a completely different universe. It was for his colleagues in the finance and commerce departments to figure out, but all they were good for was to count wads of bank notes and to issue rubber checks. Let them thrash out their abtruse problems which even the IMF experts who always lost their figures couldn't understand. And they were the troubleshooters, the international sharpshooters! Algebra was an invention of the Arabs, wasn't it? So? By Allah and all the logarithms, let the chiefs and deputy chiefs go over their little sums one more time. They had fancy offices, secretaries and designer jeans, electronic calculators which worked on batteries, and HP 41-C's! They didn't know how to use them? They typed away alongside their computers in all their pomp and circumstance? In that case, they'd be better off sharpening a pencil like in the old days before the new math, if all else failed. But that was their business, their shop, their grind!

His administration was clean—strong and clean. Who could doubt it? Who could dare claim that the police wasn't the only entity of the state embued with an iron strength? And as for international exchanges, they went far beyond any cultural mission. How could you identify the common denominator which created friendship between most of the civilized police forces and which enabled them to cooperate closely together? Maybe all officers were exempt from culture-trappings? At this point, at the end of the twentieth century when one could line up ten sturdy men and shoot a single bullet from a magnum .35 through each and every one, technology reigned in place of ideas, in place of all books. And technological progress—glory to Allah—began with the police and there found its full flowering.

Chief Mohammed remembered with exultant happiness his final degree which he had done in Paris. His French colleagues had received him most warmly like a member of the family. Pints of beer, *hallouf* ham, a workaday car, evenings spent poring through spicy dossiers full of juicy anecdotes. Not a shadow of a disagreement between the former protectee and his ex-colonizers, no, none at all. There were a couple of little tricks of the trade which yesterday's civilizers had competently, humanly transferred to him with all their well-outlined usages. He had visited many sacred spots of the French patrimony: the Eiffel tower, the Grevin museum, the police museum, the prison of Fleury-Merogis which in decreasing order of importance had been included in his training program—an integral part of this international exchange. They had even introduced him to a little blond girl as an amenity and he had done his duty like a chief. The end of racism! He had been all at once the witness, the judge and the litigant.

Times had really changed since that near-far epoch when as an adolescent, trembling with the urge to be like an Occidental and to thereby earn the title, man, he had approached a European woman at the beach (a real pizza-head), and he had been treated like a member of a sub-human species. But slaving away by the light of a ceiling bulb, he recalled the cinema-romance shud-derings and cries of this splendid creature and his heart swelled with pride and joy. Oh yes, by Allah, the transfer of powers had been accomplished painlessly, police to police. That evening Chief Mohammed drank his first whiskey with a single gulp, just like John Wayne.

And then hadn't his training began under auspicious circumstances? Who had been there, at Orly, stationed next to the turnstyle? A colleague in uniform visible to the naked eye. The chief had made his way toward him, his insignia in the palm of his hand and he had hailed him:

— Police. How's it going, buddy? Everything cool?

With a strong, virile handshake the chief passed through the turnstile. Not necessary to show his passport. How to express it? Between police officers there are no frontiers of any kind. Free passage of people and goods. And ideas. But they are probably all the same thing. At that moment the Chief of Police thought of his father. In his imagination he saw him standing before him, bridging space and time, dressed in the uniform of a colonized cop. To wit:

Primo, a khaki-colored soldier's jacket on top of an old Moroccan shirt which had neither buttons nor a collar;

Deuxio, patched-up riding shorts;

Tertio, gray puttees wrapped around his tibias;

Quarto, plain pointed leather slippers, dirty brown as dried figs.

That was what he wore day and night, all the time. And as a symbol of his authority, he carried a peasant's club. Period. Did anyone say he had a passport? Or even a cop's ID? And there he was, the chief, son of his father, nimbly traversing the frontiers (the frontiers of air no less!) of the former tutelary power! It was all very simple: Right off the bat, *illico presto*, as his Italian colleagues in the *Petit Larousse* would say, he went over to a news stand and filled up his briefcase with an armful of newspapers and magazines. Didn't matter which ones, from periodicals discussing the American recession and the stockpiling of French francs to the picture magazines dedicated to crooners and hard rockers. "Water takes the shape of the vessel which holds it" affirmed an ancient Arab philosopher, don't you see?

And on top of this, since he was a worthy trooper and well-esteemed by the pyramid of chiefs stacked above him, one day he had taken a trip on board a Boeing 747. Destination: "You-es-eh." This was for super fine training outside a city called Saint-Cinnati to perfect his methods and technology to a tee with the *Brigade anti-terroristes* ("Anti-terrorist squad" in *Amirikane*: ATS as the logo went).

One question: the chief's father—may Allah rest his soul wherever it may be—had he ever travelled any way other then on his feet, on the back of a donkey, on a bicycle or on a trolley car if necessary?

Response: no comment!

Corollary question: What would he have said if he had seen his son booked on an international flight and leaping from one civilization to another without any loss of his human dignity?

Response: Eh? . . . Oh yeah, he would have said this: "*Ya wili wili wili*! . . . Ah! Misery of our misery! Don't get into that satanic flying machine my son. Leave that to the Christians. You've got time . . ."

— Shoot again! the instructor barked at him with a nasal voice.

— Eh?

— Shoot again! Get a move on!

Standing up in front of something called Space In Vader, a sort of pinball machine with endless electronic buttons and a screen, the chief of police forced himself not to get flustered. All at the same time he had to simultaneously:

(1) Understand what the instructor in shirtsleeves said to him: he didn't speak English, he spoke American;

(2) Familiarize himself with this devilish console before actually using it;

(3) Continue with the dialogue inside his head which he was forever conducting with his Maker. Not so easy.

— Shoot again!

Good heavens, what was he supposed to shoot again? And how? When? Dizzily (even more so that his thoughts), a flying subcompact would surge forth from nothingness into the screen of the Space In Vader in a luminous arc. It never stayed in one place but instead bounced hither and thither and then disappeared as though by magic, before he could even translate the whole experience into Moroccan. And it would return, charging willy-nilly, never from the same spot, as though merely to mock him. He had to concentrate, absorb the abstract equation: subcompact=urban guerilla, foresee where these terrorist dogs were going to attack next, neutralize them in the blink of an eye by means of his intellect and his weapons. He had the submachine guns represented by the three buttons on his console. He breathed to his father: "Wait one sec'" and fired. There was a glorious shower of red sparks.

— Roger! said the instructor. You nailed him.

Yes. Roger, Dad. You see your son, you see him? Later in a conference room whose walls were entirely papered with ordinance maps with colored pins sticking into the hot points of the Arab world, Chief Mohammed assimilated American tactics and good manners and in the process never ceased his running commentary addressed to his dead father. These children of power would have never even looked at you, I swear it. You were fettered. You didn't have the uniform, you had no authority. You were nothing. In exactly the same way our brother countries were also nothing. Dog squat—at least until the day when petroleum gave them a lease on life. Roger? And to think that among his colleague chiefs, there were some whose fathers, witnesses of this non-past, were still alive! Oh, they had set them up well in beautiful villas, with servants, bathrooms and the whole works.

It's quite simple, Father: Next chance I get I'll have you rehabilitated through the intervention of higher authorities and you'll get a posthumous police merit badge, and that would be justice! All you've got to do is introduce a bill to make it law. We are all orphans . . .

At this point, right in the middle of his lovely memories, he pulled off his shirt and without opening his eyes, threw it into a corner of the cave. It was hot. In fact, it was very hot. In a regulation t-shirt, while wiggling his toes, he latched onto his American episode, and placed it into the *ad hoc* hole of the puzzle of his life of which he was so proud. And then . . . and then, he set himself to thinking about the genesis of creatures and of things.

Question: Through what aberration, as a result of what historical accident could such an uncommon man as he find himself caged in this grotto like a rat, knocking against the obstacles of these worthless dirt assholes who dared to obstruct his investigation? Could he afford to wait for the crank shaft, him? HIM? Wait for it, and put it in a state of deliquescence? But . . . but then was it central authority, the Constitution, the established powers which were in jeopardy?

Response: In a bit. I can't answer right away, I need to seriously reflect on this. Silence!

Lost in the tumbling disarray of his thoughts, covered in the dust of their falling, Chief of Police Mohammed called the Regulations captain to his aid. He didn't respond. He'd never make it to such a lost country as this one. They probably didn't even want to anyway. The chief coiled himself up on his old crate and made himself all small, naked except for his underclothes, much like a newborn babe wailing its way into this ever so complex world.

One after the other he invoked the Research and Intervention Squad, the CIA, Scotland Yard, Sherlock Holmes . . . How did those fellows manage? How did they operate in an emergency? With no telephone anywhere around, his tires flat, surrounded by hostile and illiterate peasants, not to say beatifically idiotic, an inspector who can only eat, sleep and goof off . . . and especially, an ineffable investigation which yet escapes his slightest grasp.

— Oh most powerful Allah, he prayed *in extremis*. Help me, and next year I'll make the pilgrimage to Mecca. Forevermore, I'll do my five daily prayers, and I'll never eat pork or drink liquor again. The tie was just for show. You should know what occurs in, on, and under the souls of your faithful. The long and the short of it is that I will adhere to the precepts of Islam from which I have inadvertently strayed. Here, please listen: I will recite a verse of the Koran for you . . .

And he in fact recited it, madly moving his lips. And if he added a few words of Esperanto or from some language known to him alone, nevertheless, it all worked. Hadn't the harmonious grafting of Western civilization onto the Arab Muslim world produced one of the most marvelous hybrid fruits of the century? Since Allah hadn't apparently heard him this time around, the Chief of Police finally made a big decision. He backed up at high speed, sucking in the spent exhaust. Everything had a beginning, an *alpha*.

He went back to the origin of it all: that near and distant day when, at the same time as he received a diploma illegibly signed by three different ministers (among whom was the Secretary of Agriculture, probaby to ensure the provisioning of his soul) and which was witnessed by three different seals corresponding to the reality of his functions, he had equally been graced by the foremost of all essential qualities: officiality. It was something special, ineffable, which impregnated his voice, his glance, his stance and even his clothes with a kind of ultrararified aromatic of officiousness. He who had been invested with it became at once a citizen of another planet, recognized and recognizable amongst the multitude from the moment he had the misfortune to open his mouth. Oh! He continued to use tribal words but coated them with a kind of fatty layer. Moved by the sight of a sick child, for example, he could say just as you and I would: "It can't be. He's sick. But that's silly. The poor little one." When we express ourselves in such a manner, you and me, we are easily understood by our compatriots because we're simple folk. But officials, doused in officiality, could pronounce the same words and get in response widened eyes and perked up jackal ears. That certain tone ruined everything. You'd hesitate to pass them the salt at the table when they put in a polite request. You're never quite sure if they mean to be addressing you or the salt . . . or perhaps even some invisible third interlocutor who floated a foot above your head. Startled, you twist around and look into the air but your eyes see nothing . . . and then you ask yourself: "Did he speak to me? To me? What was he talking about?"

Officiality was less visible, less obtrusive in the police force. Obligatory deception! But however disguised it may be, it was just the same there, detectable from a great distance, without radar and in degrees proportional to the hierarchical ladder. A simple cop, working the sidewalk, could stride along as though he needed a serious buffer zone of vital space; and, if he chose to speak to you, to ask you for your papers, for example, he would do it officially, breathing into the words but a fleeting meaning like ashes scattered to the winds. At the top of the pyramid, a chief, worthy of the title, could make you wait several hours in the antechamber on a bench, and when finally he'd deign to receive you, and you would begin by closing the door ever so quietly, so as not to disturb him; and you would sit down on the edge of your chair and wait expectantly: there he'd be, rereading, annotating a dossier which could well be yours, and the telephone rang and he responded with his empty voice and impatient "Hello," swiftly followed by several syllables which didn't quite correspond to any sounds you'd heard before. He hangs up, and permits his glance to fall upon your person as though asking from which planet you just landed.

— Ah, it is you, Untel? he'd start off.
— Yes, Mr. Commissioner. Forgive me.
— Tomorrow. Haven't the time. Come back tomorrow.
— Yes, Excellency.

You were so happy to get out of there and regain your freedom. He didn't threaten you. What in fact did he really say? If your superheated memory survived the office ordeal, as well as your own self, he really said something quite simple: "It's you. Come back tomorrow." Precisely like when your wife says to you on occasion, "No, dear, not tonight." You understand right way, simply through her tone of voice. Perhaps you even smile, suffused with a certain muddled indulgence. The words which just departed her lips had nothing official about them. They didn't hover beyond your grasp. They didn't frighten you.

In other State activities it was quite different. Hardly any need to disguise yourself like some vulgar cop. The closer you approach pure policy, the more pure and durable your officiality. And in your speech, you throw in a few learned phrases here, some morsels of technojargon there, some computer coordinates just to show you're up to date—all of these techniques guaranteed to pump up your man with importance and make him rise high up in the stratosphere, like a test balloon. And then there'd be a little official on your screen, a specialist as it were, fiddling with the antenna without paying the slightest attention to the quality of your reception, all so he could blow on about the so-called peasant's malaise.

— *Bismillahi rahman arrahim*! he'd start off peremptorily and pompously. In the name of the most merciful and benificent Allah . . . Three quarters of an hour later or so:

— . . . and in relation to that, there is the economic liberalism of Milton Friedman. I will talk to you about that American next week, *incha Allah*! It always seems that the Council of Ministers has just decided that promotional funds for agricultural products is endlessly in the process of being allocated, which means, maybe in several months, if that is Allah's wish. In the first place, brokerage firms are always seeking to accept cereal goods in various qualitative conditions, which implies aditional new gadgetry. Secondly, in order not to penalize animal husbandry, it has been agreed that new silos would be constructed at the sites of livestock cereal consumption. These measures tend to show that the agricultural sector would not be likely to experience further deterioration. That, in fact, one could hope for, with the aid of Allah on high: that there would be some improvement towards the end of next year . . .

Television viewers lacking a single milligram of comprehension would shout out, full of admiration:

— Ah, that one, he's smart. He knows what's what!

Those co-opted by the system, who benefitted from a few drops of oil from the big wheels, were innumerable and gravitated towards the highways and byways of power. To various degrees, they all adopted the tones and mannerisms of the big chiefs, their way of lighting cigarettes, and of talking down to those whom they administered. Even the sports reporters in the middle of a soccer match, found the time between a penalty and a goal to set up a little oil can and a lint brush for the BIG BOSS. And then there were the written symptoms of officiality, in other words, simple characters printed on paper where, in theory, you would think such affectations could least leave their stain. But then you'd be ignoring this discovery: quotation marks with which one could enclose more and more words in order to set them apart from the common lexicon. "Laxisms," mutilated syntax, a wooden language acquires a certain nobility, a certain distinction visible at first glance. To get by, you had two alternatives:

a) to ask yourself stupidly why the hell a word like "conference" or "beef" was framed by two guardian quote marks;

b) to arm yourself with a massive dictionary in an attempt to decipher the distinctions between reference and the referent of the assorted thingamajigs.

There is, of course, one other sort of reaction: to throw up one's arms and ignore it all. Which is just what I'm going to do.

But the chief was the chief. And he let nothing slip by him. Stubbornly, he redirected his thoughts into another channel. His concepts were at this point laid out in order of importance, and classified in different-colored folders. You had to do what had to be done: there must be order. And what couldn't be permitted was muddle. Having reached this level of synthesis, Chief Mohammed raised up one buttock and let loose a silent, odorless, colorless gas, and set himself to posing the real question. Here in the 1980s, what indeed was the destiny of a flesh and blood man like himself? When things get bogged down like this unholy investigation, you have to take the bull by the horns, that is, you have to lend an exemplary air to the whole discussion. No two ways about it. The issue coalesced slowly in his mind, cranial synapses no doubt impeded by the heat. But he clenched his jaws and answered himself: "national!" The solution was to examine the national destiny. For additional information, he started to run through his history, first in his maternal language, then in French so that his ideas would develop a cartesian imprint. History . . . history . . .

First there were the aboriginals, and it's hard to know just exactly what they were. Then came the Romans, all the way from Rome on the backs of elephants with their legions and aqueducts. They did what they could. They had to irrigate the country. But they spoke Latin which was definitely not an idiot's language. They were dead in any case. What's more, all they left behind were ruins like Volubilis. Later, under Mussolini, they became facists, and from the 1960s on, terrorists, what with the Red Brigade and all. One important detail which could easily be overlooked: could he, Mohammed, have become police chief during Roman times? Hardly, right?

Then there were the Visigoths . . . or the Ostrogoths? Something like that, anyway. Hordes of them. They had no police whatsoever. Let's move on to the Arabs. There was General Abderrahman and General Tariq who built the port at Gibraltar. Islamic sheikhs, marabouts, and certainly caïds. But history hadn't noted the name of a single Arab policeman. It was pretty feudal! Then there was the era of the French colonizers. If they had bothered with a few natives like his father it was only with the barest of interest. Country cops were nothing but the lackeys of imperialism. But thank the most powerful Allah, the Arabs had become free and sovereign.

At this juncture, having opened the tomb of the ages, Chief Mohammed logged the first point: who had governed the country since time out of mind? Immediate answer: a handful of individuals, an elite bracketed by quotation marks. It had dominated the silent majority and had wrung them dry financially, militarily, economically, police- and politics-wise, whether in the name of religion or civilization or perhaps we should just say, in the name of some nameless obscurity.

The chief smiled a big smile as he approached the modern era. The era which marked the dawn of national consciousness. The country was now master of its own destiny. It was represented in the O.A.U., the U.N., and by chance, in the League of Arab States; also in the Islamic Conference, which was much better because there were more Muslims than Arabs in this big world. The country was even part of the world's judicial structure! And at home (on the domestic front), the people were everywhere mass-mediatized by the television. Culture for everyone! Democracy! The least American "up-to-date" bulletin was laid out on the small screen, presto. The second indicator was obvious: who were the ones associated with power these days? People of modest origin, of middling means and simple backgrounds—the social cement between the base and the summit of the sociological pyramid. They weren't merely the sons of their fathers. Connections! They came from neither the best nor the worst schools. Ha! They were the sons of little folk with scarcely a birthright, and no heavy baggage. And they were now in command positions throughout the entire government, from the noble police force to the programming committees of radio and television. Each one of them fully wielded his own little parcel of authority. And taken all together, they disposed of real power. Any polling institute effectively handed power of determination to the people. That's a lot of progress since the days of Avicenna and Ibn Khaldun! From the days of one's infancy, when frustrated, old, illiterate granny would inundate the cradle with legends of yore to today's economic reality which contained the force of law within its strength, imagine what happiness it was to finally hold the reins of power!

He, Mohammed, son of his dead father, had the smarts, the authority, the files. During his career, he had amassed information on all kinds of people. Thus armed, he was naturally highly respected. His destiny was bound up with the nation, and secured in cement. In five years, ten at the most, he could aspire to the highest echelons in the land. And that would be justice! Imagine this: who was that Adolf ben Hitler but a nothing housepainter, of most modest means, and a son of a self-made man from the common ranks. That didn't keep him from building his little nest, bit by bit, like a bird, and finally hoisting himself to the peaks of Gotha through the force of his fist and by the sweat of his brow. He ended up dominating the entirety of Europe and he issued the call to those of his ilk, the nameless multitude, the mediocre masses. Ah, if only he had had the good sense to choose a career with the police! But no, he had been crazed. *Maboul*! He had preferred politics and the power had gone to his head . . . Unlike the police, politics wasn't just a piece of cake. It forced you to twist the most sensible thoughts, and it provoked insomnia, and even meningitis. And what's more, no politician could ever be sure at the start that his career would last very long. While the police . . .

— Hold on! the chief said suddenly to himself. Whoa! Don't budge. Stop thinking!

He had just been struck as with a whiplash by a monstrous thought, so subversive that it opened his eyes to the blinding light of reality. Frightened, breathing hard, he didn't dare follow the thought through which would have led to the most murky depths of his brain. If he had, he would probably have grabbed his gun and shot himself forthwith. And with him the whole system would have collapsed like a house of cards. It would certainly have been a disaster. A great evil. That's what comes from thinking. From behaving like an *insectual*! *Ladin mouk filousoufi*! Whore-mother, this philosophy! Thought belongs to the past. It was useless. Harmful. What could come of it but the deformation of deeds and a road to anguish? A deep understanding of human nature could make a healthy man mad. A man like the chief. And by Allah, his soul was imbued with order and method . . .

— Hey, what? What were you saying, you?
— Were you sleeping, chief? It's been a good while already.

The Chief of Police woke up for good this July 12, 1980, at approximately 1:14 p.m. according to his quartz watch. He fussed about and uprooted his thoughts, leaving no trace of them, neither somewhere in his gray matter, nor traced upon his beet-red face. **Thoughts were bad! They deserved to be** burned. Death to them! His voice, laden with pomposity, pronounced:

— Inspector Ali, listen to me well.

— Yes, chief. I think I asked you two or three questions. Of course you were probably taking little in . . .

— Just listen. While you were taking it easy . . .

— What, me! Me?

— Yes, you. You. While you were daydreaming, I considered the issue. I carefully reflected on the situation from all angles, from the front door to the roof, from A to Z as they say in French. And I have arrived at a conclusion, *sine qua non*, which is self-evident, clear and mathematical. Now hear me: it is absolutely impossible and unthinkable for me to continue this investigation in such a furnace. It isn't even my socio-economic level, or my . . . my . . . - just look at me! he suddenly cried out. Really, look at what a state I'm in.

— Yes, chief, said the inspector, wide-eyed. I've been looking at you for a good while. And you know what I see? No kidding? Sweat, everywhere. It's inhuman. Would you like me to wipe you off?

— If you like. Sure, if you like. No, no! Not with the edge of your *gandoura*. Open my traveling bag and take out a bath towel. It's clean and new. Fold it in half. Get this slush off me. It's running down my back and my belly. Go on, wipe it off. Not so hard, you onion head! I told you to rub, not scrape my skin off.

— Sorry, chief. *Ouka*, I don't know my own force. *Ouka*, it's out of my control.

— You see, inspector, we should have come here last spring. Or at least, we should have put it off until the rainy season.

— What rain? asked the inspector. It's been dry here for at least a century or two, you only have to look at the rocks of this magnificent countryside, and the heads of the local mountain folk.

— In fall or winter there should be at least a breath of air. Something cool and civilized. One couldn't stand it otherwise. If you look in my bag, you'll find a bottle of Eau de Cologne. Pour it over my head.

— O.K., chief. That sure smells good.

— It's refreshing. Does me good. I feel like a new man. You see, inspector, it's a matter of one's environment. There's an enormous difference, huge, between working in my office, and sweating here in this hole like a dead rat.

— You're right, chief. Roger-dodger. You can trust me. You're nothing like those filthy animals. So, should I go down and fill up the tires, and we'll take off? Is that it?

— No, that's not it. Hardly. You're meandering. Fantasizing.

— Whatever you say, chief. We could regain civilization in several hours, driving along with the windows down and the radio serenading our ears. Let me explain. It's a straight run down the mountain and onto the cool plains where there are supermarkets, and it's easy to find stuff to eat and drink. Just think of your air-conditioned office, and the armchair you're usually enthroned upon, which must surely be pining for you, the poor orphan! A far cry from that old crate you're sitting on now. Your ass must be bruised, that's what I think. Think of your rank, chief! *Achourfa wal karam*, like they used to say in the days of the Caliphs: "Nobility and human dignity." That counts for something.

— Hmmm! said the chief. Hmmmm!

— Clearly! the inspector went on with the rigorous dialectic certified by the S.G.D.G. . . . Clearly. The nobility of the armchair determines the human dignity of the one who is seated in it, just as a succulent meal like *hargma* or *mhencha* promotes the dignity of your stomach. Not to mention how joyous is the digestion of a *Pasha*. A simple plate of beans could never accomplish that. Never!

— Hmmm, repeated the chief. Your logic has the odd odor of a kitchen to it, but there are a few good planks in it. Probably laminated, I'd say. Now, tell me, what about the suspects?

— Those dolts? It's quite simple, chief: If the Prophet stalked courageously up to the mountain, the mountain will come to you in the form of a truck. After all, we're in the twentieth century.

— How's that? I'm not following you.

— We send up those peasants in a flash, *fissa*. Our cohorts in the army could round them up in a military truck. They're used to it, you know, drumming up those rural crowds for the big occasions in town. Once in the city, the investigation could proceed of its own accord. No more heat, no more discomfort, no oriental backbreakers!

The chief stayed silent for a moment,, and then said:

— Do you see the word *sucker* tatooed across my forehead, or even written in kohl?

— Neither, chief, I was very surprised by your . . .

— Do you really think, *reeeally* think that I hadn't already thought of this feeble solution? This fantasy?

— By Allah and the Prophet, did you really? YOU? How did you manage that? What happened?

— I started to get a migrain. Just the start of one, because I immediately gave up the idea. I gave no desire to stuff myself full of aspirin. I'm strictly opposed to all drugs. When an idea is out of place, I drop it. That's the way I am.

— You're lucky, chief, the inspector exclaimed, his eyes wide open.

— I'm tired of spelling everything out for you. You can't tell the difference between a sausage and a razor to cut your throat with. It's a matter of regulations! That's the difference.

He looked the inspector up and down and finished, peremptorily,

— *Voila!*

— I don't see the evidence, said the inspector tentatively. I truly don't. By Allah and the Prophet.

— So you don't understand? Well, I'm going to knock on your stupidity with a scotch hammer made in *Idenbara*. Listen carefully to me. I was ordered to come investigate here. Here, and not in town in my office. And certainly not in a supermarket. Here, in this filthy, boiling countryside which is like being in the baths. And to bring my official mission to its conclusion, to the final dot of the 'i' in the file. Get it?

— No. Not at all. If I understand you, the front door is closed. There isn't even a door. You're backed into a corner, chief. You can't investigate here, on the spot, because it's like a furnace. And I empathize with your physical and moral aches and pains. And you can't transport the peasants home, I mean to the city, either, so you could interrogate them properly. Under these circumstances, there's something which doesn't fit. I don't know if you could say that the serpent is eating its own tail, but you might as well say that the investigation is faltering, bogged down and . . .

— Listen, you.

— Yes, but I'm scared that you're going to get all angry at me, and, unthinkingly, from some vital need, against adversity itself. But I see with great pleasure that your face has lightened up. That must mean that you've just had a fortuitous thought which might help you out of this mess. Quickly give me the good news.

— Open my bag and get me a proper shirt.

— O.K., chief. With pleasure. So what about this idea?

— You should never get lost in the details, pronounced the chief in a most stentorial tone. It's a question of circling the problem from above as though you're in a reconnaisance plane. Like that, you've got all the elements under inspection. It's logical. I don't know if you have realized it, but you and I have become democratized. At the end of this century, you and I will be complete equals. Transformations within continuity, of course. Do you follow me?

— No. Not at all. I never get involved in politics.

— I'm not talking about politics, but about reality. Social reality. Here, let's take a completely silly example: Who is presently here, right now in this unhappy cavern?

The inspector turned on his heels. He swept the cavern with a single glance and said somewhat hebephrenetically:

— No one but us two, chief. I don't see anyone else.

— Who, us two?

— Well, you, chief, and me.

— That's right, said the chief, approvingly. No one but us two. Let's examine more closely: there is a chief and a subordinate. A chief like me has great responsibilities. By dint of circumstances, I'm going to show right now the ins and outs of democratizations. Come closer.

— Is it serious, chief?

— Sit down close to me. Closer. Lister: I am going to permit myself to share my responsibilities in this investigation with you.

— By Allah . . .

— Yes, Inspector Ali. My comrade, my friend. It's proof of the confidence which I am democratically placing in you. I hope, and feel confident, that you will be worthy of it. So listen: Up in high places, some top secret information surfaced indicating that there is a dangrous subversive, a Moroccan citizen, who lived for a long time in Europe, and who has illegally crossed into the country last week. He's here, in this village.

— By Allah and the Prophet!

— Yup. The State's police don't make mistakes. They have ears everywhere and they work hand in hand with the forces of over thirty countries. At all costs we must find this criminal and lock him up as soon as possible.

The inspector mentally reviewed the members of the Ait Yafelman family, from Raho right down to the two cinnamon-colored twins.

— Is it a man? he asked apprehensively.

— I said a subversive. Not a *subversette*. I know my language.

— Praise Allah! exclaimed the inspector.

— Why praise Allah?

— Oh, it's nothing. A private matter between me and myself. How old is this terrorist?

— Between thirty and thirty-five years.

— Just like you, then?

— What's that? Oh, I suppose so. Although there's nothing subversive about me. We don't know his name. But he is native to this region. And what's more, he must speak European. Try to catch him in that. You're talkative, and kind of clever. And because of your proletarian roots, you're closer to these dirt-asses than I am, like a fish in a school. So consequently, I am giving you an official mandate to run the investigation on a provisional basis. What do you say about that, inspector?

The inspector thought hard about it, and bounded up the staircase of options and alternatives four steps at a time. He composed his face instantly into the inscrutability of a retard, and said:

— Uhh ...

— That sends you for a loop, doesn't it? I told you we are in the era of democratization! Go on, inspector, express your deepest feelings. This is a red letter day. Go to it, comrade, express your joy.

— I don't know if I quite dare, chief.

— Dare! Dare! Don't worry. We are equals, you and I.

— You see, chief, I am literally crushed by the honor which you have just placed upon my shoulders. It's too much.

— I believe I specified that it would be provisional.

— I heard you. But, even provisionally, this honor caught me off-guard. My innards are all knotted up. I don't know what it is, chief, but ordinary people have no desire to assume their responsibilities. It gets them all worked up. And that's not just since yesterday.

— What are you blithering about? Explain yourself!

— Willingly, chief. It's very simple: have you ever seen a nobody become a king or a president?

— Who was telling the *Arabian Nights*?

114

— Nobody, chief. That's why I am quite logically noting that it's quite impossible. These days, fairy tales aren't selling. On the other hand, the B.D.! I regret to inform you, dear chief, that I am declining your offer, generous and disinterested as it was.

The chief almost blew up for the third or fourth time that day, but he contained himself. Blocked, foiled in his investigation, he sought to reestablish his position. He said very gently, even amiably:

— Are you refusing an order?

— So the offer has now become an order? the inspector asked expressionlessly.

— Of course it's an offer—tinged with a certain . . ., a certain . . ., it's a concession, that's the precise word.

— Even gift-wrapped, I cannot accept it, chief.

— But why not? Why the hell not, you spare tire?

— Because you're the one. You're the one who was invested with this official mission. I'm just an assistant. There are no responsibilities outlined in my portfolio. You never stop telling me that my job is to carry out orders. Implement. That's all. Rules are rules. I neither can, nor wish to contravene them. I'm not crazy. Naive, maybe, but not crazy.

The cerebral mechanics of the Chief of Police had been reacting like convulsive compressors for quite some time now. His past had been full of such luminous successes: so many satisfactorily completed investigations, so many arrests, so many good efficiency reports! The future was now menacing: the total fiasco on this mountain, for starters, and . . . and . . . all because of some obscure peasants, and this stupid bread-oven guard's son for whom he felt such disdain!

— My brother, started the chief, forgive me for my mistakes. If by chance I've done wrong by you in the past, you mustn't hold me to account. I have a Mediterranean disposition, and besides, it's so hot out here. You know, I quite like you.

— Amen, the inspector concluded. How much will you give me?

A spent match was lying on the floor. He picked it up.

— What's that?

— What are you offering me in the event that I might eventually direct this investigation in your stead?

— But you're not doing it in my stead! Out of the question!

— Well, then, nothing's settled. I am a faithful servant of the State. Either you apply the regulations, or don't come running to me. It's your decision. You're the chief.

With his thumbnail, he folded the match stick in two, lengthwise, and began to slowly, carefully, pick his teeth. He had time.

— Listen here, said the chief.

— I'm listening.

— It goes without saying that we will both sign the investigation brief. Your name will be on all the papers. Moreover, you'll get promoted right away. Lest you forget, this is important business.

115

— I'm an Arab, chief, and African on top of that. If I've picked up a bit of civilization, it's been in the most concrete manifestations. For example, I know that *souk* means market, and vice-versa. As for the abstract, well, it's like the wind to me. The sons of the desert know that the scirocco or the *simoun* blows up above their heads. There's nothing more to it than that.

In a space between two incisors, he had just extracted something which seemed to astound him. Could it possibly be a piece of meat?

— What do you want, after all, a mountain of beans? the chief exclaimed.

— *Ouka* yourself, don't get antsy. Remember, we are having a democratic, amiable conversation. I remember one time, the barber in the *medina* was determined to shave all my hair off with his cabbage cutter, leaving zero! I said to him ... Oh, what do I want, chief? Not much. The regulations expressly state ...

— Enough! O.K., the chief screamed. You have full authority. Carte Blanche for the duration of the investigation.

Ali brought the sliver of meat up to his mouth: you mustn't waste anything in the Third World. He threw away the match: it was useless. He said:

— I am most grateful, chief. But we're no longer in the middle ages when a man's word sufficed. Alas, we're living in the twentieth century of iron, where everything must be written down.

— My word should be enough for you, you son of a dog!

— For me, yes. In the 15th, or even the 19th century, I would have accepted it unwaveringly, good as gold. But there are, these days, fluctuations, exchange rates. So, like all currencies, a man's word has a floating rate. And then there's that stupid rule which states specifically that under these circumstances that everything must be written down, article 3, line vii. Therefore, I need a written executive order signed by your hand, as chief. You should have all the necessaries in your sack: pen, correct formulas, stamp, and all that.

They talked this way and that for a long time, bickering over all possible points, and they almost came to blows. Obstinate, the inspector didn't budge one Greek iota. He knew the law, and some cousin's or concierge's ersatz law; and he hadn't any intention of violating it, even with a bit of vaseline on hand; even he, who had often been the acrobat of the *medina* and of police conventions. But since he stood to gain from it, he changed his tune and intended to stay what he was, a simple inspector with no responsibilities and, *incha Allah*, with no future... He got what he wanted in the end.

— Here's your scrap of paper! (His voice was curiously husky.) Are you happy now, crocodile head?

— By Allah and the Prophet, you're asking me that?

— So it's agreed!

They shook hands. The chief's was clammy.

Equitably and in silence, they shared the fevered sandwiches, the thermos

116

of coffee, a sticky glob of what had once been chocolate, and some oranges whose juice and peels Ali nimbly consumed. He shot the seeds straight out in front of him with the strength of a llama spitting. One of them hit the chief right in the eye. Chewing away, the inspector thought about a nine-course meal: my goodness, but there were good things in the country, as surely as eight and nine make . . . exactly how much? Suddenly, he felt as if his promotion could only advance his prospects with his two future wives, the mere memory of whom tingled his loins. By instinct he would have to follow the trail, trusting his luck instead of reason. The chief, neutralized for the moment, had indeed been driven back into his lair, tail between his legs. Would that Allah, in his infinite compassion, continue to heat the sun to a white brightness, and to let loose hell's temperatures on this mountain. Thank you, Allah! Praise to You! . . . And as for the big chiefs in the force, even if they had correctly read and interpreted the coded information on the computer consoles at Head-quarters, there was a way to correctly utilize the info. And Inspector Ali knew how to pull the threads together, and unravel the knots. And, what was this case anyway? A terrorist *here*, here among these Koranic mountain folk? Strange. Very strange!

They had another day and a half of hospitality remaining, at most 48 hours. Lots of time, by Allah and the Prophet. He was going to conduct this investigation his own way: climb down the rungs of the hierarchy, instead of climbing on the backs of others. You could drag a donkey with a rope, but you couldn't push him with it. You couldn't force him to drink if he wasn't thirsty. The officials above him had no say in it at all. They had nothing to do with it, but they weren't clowns. They dealt only with orders, restraints, and fear. And he hadn't been hatched during the last bit of nonsense. Roll him up in flour like conger eel? He knew that the chief had telephoned upstairs to his brain. He knew it with scientific certainty. This species of gnat had shown by his attempted ruse that he knew he was cornered amongst the peasants from whom he could get nothing more that a wisp of straw; that his subordinate was going to step forward and do his dirty work, like some recent immigrant; and that once the investigation was terminated, he would make up some report on him which would do away with him, liquidate him forever. Chiefs were all like that. All for themselves, nothing for the others, and their word was worth less than a fart, whether oral or written.

Horns were locked. They were joined in battle, like Carter and Khomeini. Who would win? The Islam of the Middle Ages, or the technology of the *Lamerikanes*? The inspector laid all bets on the old Patriarch of Qom. He had said he'd have the Shah's skin, and he'd gotten it. And he'd get the pre-sident's. And he, the inspector, he fought the chief on his own terms. His name was Ali like anyone's, son of a poor oven guardian and a maid who had known no joy, or earthly life here down below. Ali was now among his own, enveloped by *his* tribe, and endowed with full powers.

— *Allah Akbar*, he intoned sonorously.

— That's right, approved the chief. May Allah help you during this perilous mission. Do honor to your chief.

The inspector rose from the floor like an Ayatollah and departed, murmuring thanks to the Lord. There were tears in his eyes.

9

At the end of the afternoon, he knew the village stone by stone. Who could claim that he hadn't been born there and lived there all his life? Right away, he had hurried over to Hajja, his heart expansive and greetings warm.

— Hajja, oh Hajja, he had said to her, salivating wildly. I'm so happy to see you, and to chat a few moments with you! Right up to nightfall, if Allah wills it. Would you like me to light your fire? Where does that take place? I know how to knead the dough and cook the bread in the old-fashioned way. Hajja, little mother, something terrible has happened. The adult with all 32 teeth whose name is Mohammed, known as the chief, has been whacko since birth. Obviously his father was a cop—*scur-ty**—in the employ of the Christians. And then, since Independance, as they call it, he became *scur-ty* himself but a chief *scur-ty* if you can believe it! There's the big difference. He's all spaced out. He's dingy! Either that or he's touched by the *kouriyya*, the black fever from Sudan. Or that he's wandering around in his head somewhere. What's more, he can't take the least bit of spring sun, like today's gift of Allah's sunshine. He tried to tell me that there was some dangerous criminal wandering around this village! What do you think of it, Hajja?

— What are you talking about?

— It's not me, grandmother. It's him with his loose mouth.

— What is this specious lie? This unmentionable?

— It's the chief. The plains are the plains, cities are cities, and unbelievable things go on there. Frankish civilization must have turned his head, that's clear. There's nothing indigenous left in him, as there is in you and me. You tell me it's nonsense, and I believe you. By Allah and the Prophet, I am

---

*Here, the author is playing with the Moroccan deformation of the French national secret police, *La Sûreté*.

greatly reassured by you. I, who stand here talking with you, have always known how to put the wheat with the wheat, the dogs with the dogs, and the lies in the trash. It's nothing but word crap. Through what Herculean feat could there possibly be subversion on this grand mountain, I ask you?

— What's subversion?

— There are those who say that it is the door which leads to liberty; others say it's a prison door. Who knows? Listen, little mother, let us speak of serious things, since neither you nor I were born yesterday, nor are we nuts. In the name of most merciful and benificent Allah, tell me their names.

— What names? Stop spouting nonsense. You'll end up giving me the staggers.

— You think my heart is not trembling? In the human heart which Allah gave me? Here's the story, Hajja: I walked up the path earlier. I had just been having a nice conversation with Raho. I wan't thinking about anything, and I was all quiet inside: spleen, lungs, liver, the whole works. And then . . . and then, what did I see before my eyes, close enough to touch? Two *houries*, two temptresses come down from paradise, wrapped in beauty, grace . . . they must be illusions, right?

— Yasmine and Yasmina? My grand nieces?

He immediately picked her up in his arms and kissed her on both cheeks, the forehead and her hair. She smelled good, like cloves, like truth, like naivete. He set her back on the ground, and began a pirouette with her in a mad dance. She resisted a bit, laughed, happy and agèd.

— Yasmine, Yasmina. Yasmina, and Yasmine! My word of honor, those are names I particularly like! They couldn't have any others.

— Let me go, stop . . . stop!

Hajja's laugh was like an orchestra of fifes and cymbals.

— This day is my joy, the inspector cried out. Bless Allah. I thank Him for having created them, from birth to my last breath, I shall render hommage to him. I ask myself how He managed . . . to make them just so, with such perfection, fashioned by His august hand! Once or twice in my life as an Arab I've had the chance to admire Jasmine flowers. Heavens, but they're pretty. Their scent is intoxicating. I've got good eyes. And so they're your great nieces! Give me your hand so I can kiss it like it deserves. By what abberation did I fail to see them last night? It's true it was dark, but their beauty would have dazzled me from way off, in a blinding flash.

— Your had your nose stuck in the tagine stew, she said.

— It was delicious, Hajja! I'll remember it for the rest of my life. For that as well, I bless you. So, here's the story: it's impossible for me to choose one over the other. They are equally wonderful. And besides, I wouldn't want to separate them. Do you understand, little mother?

— No, Hajja said in all innocence.

— I was perfectly happy in my little life, moving along from day to day. Neither a chief nor a nothing. Pretty much a free and sovereign Arab, as they say. But you don't bother with *boulitiks*, do you? You're quite right. I even got married so I wouldn't end up a poor lonely soul. Formerly, my wife was younger, more fresh and wholesome, like good fresh oats. Hajja, I swear to you, cities wear people down. Whatever you do, don't go live in one. It makes women scabrous and scroffulous, and dries them out from the inside— juiceless, if you know what I mean. But you're far from being a man. Born like you, in the country, my wife one day found herself in a little cinderblock (those are fake stones) apartment where all she could do was turn around in circles, and wait. For what? We'll see. Tomorrow, *incha Allah*, I will repudiate her, and send her back to her native hamlet, at least if it hasn't been bought by the Club Mediterranée, and made all *exotik* for the *touriskes*. Oh, yes, I would have done better to live with my solitude. Patience is a Koranic virtue, yes or no?

— What are you talking about, my son? Hajja slowly asked.

She had one eye half closed, and the other wide open.

— Of my desolate life, he cried out, in the depths of his depression. I'm cursed. What has been my harvest these long years, besides my wife who hardly ever makes love, and bawls me out all the rest of the time? My work! You want me to tell you? You want to know what my work in the government is all about? It's dog's play. That's all. Shadow people and arrest them. People I don't know from Adam, and who've never done anything to me. What crap! And when I return home, there's not even anything to eat, or if there is, it's revolting. So here's my chief dragging me around so's I can arrest one of your people. He's crazy. One of these days, I'm going to trail my own shadow and arrest myself. Oh, I'm so unhappy.

Two or three minutes earlier, enthusiasm and desire had literally lifted him thirty centimeters off the ground. Now, his face was crumpled and creased by streams of tears. To the naked eye, his sincerity was absolutely genuine.

— Calm yourself, said Hajja, taken aback by the depth of his feelings. Calm down a bit, my son of the plains. You're not yet an orphan to yourself.

Standing up rigidly, he looked through the old woman as if she were made of glass, and mumbled a verse from the Koran which he had painfully learned by heart in early childhood:

— I will not swear by this country—I will leave this country—I will depart from my descendants and my forebears—Man is so . . . so miserable . . .

— Amen, Hajja finished, kissing his left shoulder. Now stop, my son. Your mistake was in dreaming about the Caliphs long since in their tombs. Allah forgives you.

— It's my only heritage, Hajja. I've confused it with civilization and the police. Luckily, I don't understand *hard rock* at all. Say "yes". Make me happy, give me joy. Say "yes" right away.

— Yes, she answered immediately, without understanding. Yes what? What are you talking about now?

— About my engagement to Yasmine and Yasmina. I'm well off. I've got formica furniture. It's a kind of brilliant, blue wood, blue as the sky right above our heads. I'll give you a gift of an armchair made of naugahyde which is leather, but better than animal leather. You'll see. You'll be as happy as you deserve, sitting it it. As for the rest, I'll sell that stuff off in the *souk*: casseroles, toilet seats, bidets, heating gas, doors, windows, television, bathtub. I'll sell them all off, and empty my savings account and my account in the bank. That way, I'll have some cash and I'll be happy. That's not even counting the pension funds the government will owe me, unless they renege and lose the grace of Allah. This is what I'm going to do: I'll resign my commission and come to live here among you all. I'm a peasant who wandered off into the police by accident. As the Koran says, I'll never again swear by the godless city, I'll abandon that tower of Babel...

— Stop, stop. You're blaspheming.

— You don't know the city, Hajja. If you did, you'd also curse it. The houses on the village square? I'll buy them. That's easy when you've got some wherewithal. You say they are falling apart, and there are only a few standing walls? Well, I've got two arms, and two hands as well! One house for you, one for Raho, and one for me and my two wives. Like that, we'll be one happy family. If I were you, little mother from my past, I wouldn't hesitate an instant before such a luminous, sunny future. And anyway, I'm young and handsome. Say "yes."

Hajja had lowered her head, and seemed to be counting the pebbles between her naked feet. Without any expression, she said:

— You should have told me all this last night... or even this morning.

— Why, are my fiancées promised to someone else?

— No, oh no!

— So then?

She remained silent for a long moment, with her eyes lowered, wiggling her toes. Then she said:

— You should speak to Raho about it. At the Village Council.

And she added in a trembling voice:

— There will be a big feast.

— Ah, that's why the Ait Yafelman got out their drums and other instruments this morning.

— Ah... ah, yes, she breathed.

He squeezed her in his arms and kissed her on the head. She smelled of paradise.

— The Lord is blessed! By Allah and the Prophet, I swear this day is my new beginning. To be engaged, a total change of existence, a pantagruelian feast awaits me this evening, song and dance... Touch my heart, Hajja: it's bubbling away so furiously, it's about to burst. I was right to come here, believe me. Destiny is mighty. In the name of Allah the most merciful and benificent, master of the worlds and king of the last judgment, I ask you, I ask all of you for your hospitality forever. Ever and ever.

Sobbing,, Hajja put one foot in front of the other, one after the other, and slowly, like a sleep walker, she gently fled. The inspector was sure and certain she cried from joy.

— She's sensitive, he said to himself. I go too far. I'd make a cow cry.

And the investigation? Ah, yes, the investigation . . .
Report:
— It's moving along, chief. The trail is hot, it rolls of its own accord. Real soon now. Don't you worry about it any more . . .
— How can you take it? asked the chief, who seemed each hour to melt away further.
— What's that?
— How can you deal with such a furnace? Are you made of stone, or what?
— It's a question of skin and equilibrium, chief. That's clear. And then, I'm going to eat well tonight. Do you understand?
— No.
— The mere thought of it gives me wings to fly and a ten out of ten professional awareness of my duty. All hardship deserves its rewards—and, in the prospect, oh what a reward! Fine. Right away, chief. A quarter hour to kill. Don't move. Don't start your head pounding.

He snapped off a military salute, and turned on his heels. Nimbly. This chief wasn't worth a rusty nail. Only yesterday, surrounded by the artificial aura of his power, he had been a martinet. A whole box of tools rattling around and banging away, mother fucker! And what was he now? A deflated bag of wind, an empty goat skin, a mere rag of a man. By the grace of Allah, Inspector Ali wasn't going to put off saying to him: "Mohammed, take your shirt and wipe my feet." In his fevered enthusiasm, while he wandered in search of another chat with a member of the Ait Yafelman, he started telling the beautiful story of modern times adapted to the sauce Haroun-Arrachid, improvising as best he could from his overflowing natural generosity: and if . . . And if, due to the effect of the sun, the statues came loose from their pedestals and tumbled down? Melted bolts, *voilà*, no more statues. Didn't bolts from car wheels sometimes come off while one was driving? The car veers, smashes up, and History changes its course and its allegiance; isn't that so? "Well," he thought. And he burst out in laughter.

Well, let's suppose, in seriousness, that those chiefs, big and small as they may be, are relieved by circumstance (a road accident, a kind of technological magic, an unpredictable and sudden change of History) of their nuts and bolts and found themselves between one day and the next in the caves of this mountain? What would they do? How would they assert themselves and what would they say? Of course, they certainly would try to insist on being taken at their own face value. But no one would see them that way, nor take them seriously. Hajja surely would tell them: "Get out of here. *Roh! Fissa!* Go play with your teeth and don't tell me tales." The inspector, laughing, slapped his thighs. No, they couldn't impose upon any of these peasants who would not recognize them for what they really were, who had never seen them in their native glory—and couldn't care less.

Then, the laughter strangled in the inspector's throat. He slowed his steps and said aloud:

— You, are you crazy?

— Yes, he answered, quite crazy. I can't stop thinking about those two young girls. It's making me delirious.

His shadow had turned with the sun. It was now to his left and was slowly stretching as he walked. He stared at it with fear. But no! never had one seen a tumbled statue, at least not in this country that was ignorant of even the meaning of revolution. "Ali, were they blind and nuts, those guys who hired you in the police? How ever did you get through the gauntlet? Of all devils, what was he scheming in his head? The revolution? All by himself? "I was at peace, he thought. I had a good police job. Something sure, with a paycheck at the end of the month. A slow and painful promotion but I am far from being old. I was working, more or less, as I felt like it. I occasionally got angry inside with all the things that put me off. But I didn't think about it much. I DID NOT THINK. Chief Mohammed is right to say that the *insectuals* are sick in the head."

He stopped. He raised his hand to his brow. How hot it was. Feverish. In a minute he was going to crack. Various conflicting elements were battling with blows between his eyebrows and his hairline, centrifugal and centripetal forces and forces with other qualifiers which he couldn't name, all creating a racket in his skull like tumblers: Yasmine and Yasmina, the return to the earth, the investigation that had only just begun, his good wife, the chief and the whole damn police force, and the sense of duty which collared you in any God-forsaken place—and the State which would not let him gambol about like a kid inside an inspector's skin. How could he save himself? Who would show him the way? So thirsty, who would quench his need of truth and salvation? In a word, how could he pull off an escape from this mess?

Before he had become civilized on the installment plan, when he was still an adolescent, homeless and worthless, he had had to think up perverse schemes to survive, acting instinctively, like a cow chewing and ruminating the same mouthful of straw for hours. One single idea at a time, that was his style. When the idea was consumed like a liquorice stick, he spit it out in the gutter and started out on another. Patience led to peace, to *baraka*.

As alien and strange as it may be, the contribution of the West had slowly forced him to bring together in his head, all at once, many solutions to a given problem and, at the moment of decision, to reach a golden mean: one quarter goat, one quarter cabbage, the rest a bit of broth holding it all together. If the final product did correspond to what his bosses expected of him, it wasn't his doing. A miracle no doubt, a mathematical proof that Allah coexisted with administrative waste paper and accommodated himself to the sense of order borrowed from the Christian West. Things had to be such since Ali was Ali. To a subordinated position corresponded an inferior reaction. This philosophy of the golden mean had kept him in work—and alive. He was fine where he was, neither high nor low. What could come from ambition but a mass of responsibilities and an overload for his poor brain? Was he not a perfect optimist, a "raving liberal" who couldn't consider the future (Oh! no, under no circumstances! It was too complex. One ought rather cover one's face and navigate blindly), but instead just reconsider minutely his past—and that of his compatriots who hadn't changed a bit? Well, in that case, then! He was quite lucky!

— Let's see, he thought on this day, the twelfth of July, 1980, in the middle of the afternoon, with the wide sky for witness. Well. I cannot ruminate a single idea as in the good old days. And I will end up in a padded cell if I continue to think of too many things at the same time, that's for sure. It might be Christian but it's not Muslim. Clean out your head, Ali.

He had the rare ability to liberate his mind at will. And that's what he did instantly. That is, he dipped his hand in the pocket of his long sleeveless shirt, took out a coin and bet against himself by Allah and the Prophet that:

1) Tails: He would take the straight and narrow path, would seriously conduct the investigation insofar as it was possible . . . Let us not let go of the prey for its shadow and the dog's tail for its teeth.

2) Heads: He would make love and peace to his dying days. At least, mostly, inasmuch as possible.

Shutting his eyes, he tossed the coin in the air. He never did find it in spite of all his searches on his knees, under the stupefied stare of four or five urchins who stood motionless at a distance. Was it possible that one of them was able to move faster than Western thought, and grab it in the air no less? But maybe the sand was, after all, sand, as it should be, abundant and fine-grained, unyielding to archeological digs. So, he considered a third solution: quickly flee to the car, flat tires and all, drive it on the wheel-rims if need be until he reached the first phone booth, and urgently request a new chief who, for Allah's sake, would unflinchingly tolerate the heat and these peasants coming directly from the Middle Ages. As for Chief Mohammed, for heaven's sake and in the name of a merciful and benevolent Allah, let them come and take him in a helicopter. Let them bring a stretcher and paramedic gear! Quick, quick, quick! Everything was messed up inside him: his brain, his spleen, the state.

— What great reasoning, the inspector congratulated himself.

Smiling from ear to ear, he rubbed his hands as if washing them. And he concluded, in his inner heart, but with conviction:

— Tomorrow. Maybe even tonight, after dinner. I have plenty of time. Nothing pressing. One thing at a time.

He added in French, paraphrasing rather than quoting:

— That "*Oxyde-de-dents,*"* he's crazy, by Allah! Still busy! and for this he has gone away from home!"

---

*The author here offers a personal note: "I, like Inspector Ali, am always confused by concepts: could they indeed be chemical products, or, the Occident?" The pun in French then, if outrageous, proffers dental hygiene, Western values oxidizing Islamic ones, and one could go on . . .

Kifech doesn't understand. Someone had said to him . . . Who had asked him to shut up? He didn't remember. There was too much clutter in his head. And what had he been told, in fact? Ah yes! "Listen, Dictionary. Don't go opening your big . . ." Alright, he isn't deaf. He knows this phrase by heart. He has been told it ten times. No, twelve times. He has counted the times on his fingers.

But why do they call him Dictionary, the Wise One? His name has been Kifech* as far back as he could remember. Of course, he knew things. So why keep them to himself? It's not fair. This man who enters caves and comes out at every turn, is looking for something. That's obvious. He inspects, he questions. He laughs, talks to himself. Kifech could help him. He has a great experience of life. He has been to the city, he has worked there. In all kinds of short jobs. He was fired from them all. And why? He had never done any harm.

Doorman at a hotel, with a nice uniform. The only suit he had ever had. Barely a week. No, ten days. Before that . . . Yes, those were the good old days, he had a little stall in the *medina*, where he sold lemonade. To attract patrons he had bought a radio. Almost a piece of furniture. At dawn he would turn it on, full blast, clockwise. It was simple. He turned it counter-clockwise only late at night, when he was really tired. They sure were cheerful, those popular tunes! tambourines, lutes, flutes, fifes, refrains repeated in a chorus while clapping hands. The lemonade bottles vibrated on their rack, and Kifech would scream out the catch phrase with all his heart. Why did the neighbors threaten him with their fists? And what did they tell him so loudly? A bit more and they would have stoned his radio. But he had saved it. He had placed it on his shoulders and had left the city one day, had gone straight to his native mountain, without even bothering to close up his stall. Those folks from down there didn't like joy, that's for sure. They drank their lemonade and then screwed up their faces. Ah yes! how had he carried the radio through fields, roads, railways, and hills? He couldn't even remember. That was so distant now. But the radio was still there, in the cave where he lived with his parents and brothers and sisters. There was no more music, though, no matter how he turned the knobs, all of them. Morning and night. Maybe the thing only worked in the city? . . .

Had he previously worked in the PTT? Him? How could he remember the details of such a full life? They had told him . . . they had explained ("I know," he had answered immediately. "I know.") in the mountain and he, Kifech, a mountain man, who knew the area ("Yes, I know, I was born here. I know.") could follow the telephone cable in the ditches and the cedar forest ("I know, that's easy."); maybe the cable had fallen and broken, in which case here were the tools to fix it: "I know," he had concluded. And he went on cheerfully. Much later the telephone still didn't work. Yet, Kifech had

*Kifech means "What?" "What's that?" It is a surname. (Author's note)

done what was necessary with a big string . . .

Kifech didn't understand the world. Why did the Ait Yafelman have to live like tracked animals? Why need they renounce everything? It seemed that they were hiding, but from whom or what? As far back as he could remember, he could see only flight, heels raising dust. Why, as she goes past him, does Hajja quickly raise her finger to her lips? What's the secret? By Allah, what is it that he must not say?

Away from children and adults, in order to be able to play the crucial game, Bourguine had traced a circle in the sand with his finger, had sat down inside the circle as if to settle the boundaries of his meditation, and had taken a card deck out of nowhere. The minute before his hands had been open, palms down, side by side at eye level. He lowered them, closed them and, when he opened them again, a fan-shaped wheel of cards appeared.

He shuffled them, shuffled them again in a spiral, then cut them. They lay in two equal stacks, a foot apart. Now the trial was to begin. He had never succeeded before. Usually, when he played poker with himself (against his perfect alter ego), he did so in perfect equity: his right hand was his own, his left hand was that of an invisible and therefore all the more present partner. Most often he would win, against his will, without cheating. He was ambidextrous. Occasionally, it was the other who would carry off the stakes, stakes he handed over without a grudge—from the left pocket. Such was the game. Bad luck, too.

Did fate conceal chance? One had to check. Test it. He had been thinking about it since the previous night, after having received Raho's instructions. One trick for him, the right hand. The second for . . . yes, for Allah. Of course, that was blasphemy: the Sublime Creator was not a trickster, he had no need for three of a kind or a flush to issue his decrees. He had expressly forbidden gambling in his Book. But this native from the city was quite congenial, *simpatico* in his simplicity. There was no evil in him. He had even asked in marriage his own twin sisters. Hajja had said, and repeated, that he was sincere. She knew human nature. But Raho only trusted the stars. They had more permanence than mere mortals.

So, two equal piles of cards, quite level, no way to guess. One contained death. If the first card came from Allah's side, then to him belonged Destiny as in all times. In case of the contrary, he had to obey Raho's orders. The old mountain man had consulted the stars. He knew what he was doing.

Slowly, almost regretfully, he took up the first card, turned it over: *ten of hearts*. And on the side of Providence? What was there? The *ace of diamonds*. Never had Raho been wrong. He drew his divinations from the earliest Antiquity. A kind of science of which he sometimes spoke. It was the only legacy he had inherited from his ancestors. Maybe all depended on the third card. Red, or black?

A shadow suddenly stretched over him and a cheerful voice called out:

— Ah! Greetings, Bourguine! I was looking for you.

Before turning, even before being startled, Bourguine knew that the card was that of death. He pried up just a corner, took a peek, then shook his head. It was decreed. Too bad.

— Greetings, my brother, he answered.

Inspector Ali sat down cross-legged and continued as if he were picking up a conversation interrupted by a slight incident. Whether it be with Hajja, Bourguine or someone else, by Allah and the Prophet, it was all the same! Did he talk more than he listened? Really? And did anyone in this village ever work? Did anyone have any kind of occupation? Ali resembled in no way Chief Mohammed so he was not about to ask stupid questions such as: was there a factory a mile around, or at least a little mill of some sort? If unemployment checks never reached this mountain, were, in fact, actually unknown in name as well as significance, then by what did they live? You say, my brother, that today there was enough to avoid starving and thanks to Allah for that? Fine, thank Allah for providing food for the birds, but what about tomorrow? Have you thought about the future in this merciless century? I do know that fall follows summer, that's given. Maybe even the rainy season . . . Ah! A few acres of land would be sown, then *incha Allah*? In mid-sentence he shouted point-blank:

— You speak French, traveler? *Habla spañol, protuguese, youspik l'amerikane cuba jawohl da*?

— Is your throat dry, my brother? said Bourguine.

— It's not you! concluded the inspector, sighing in relief. I am happy. I was also telling myself . . .

And without further ado, he came to the meat of the matter. Here is the story: the coin had been lost, possibly in the bloody sand, but possibly in the pocket of one of those idle loafers. To top it all, he didn't even know on which side it had fallen. Heads or tails? Who could guess? He did have other coins but didn't wish to toss them. The right moment had passed, he had lost his inspiration. To avoid the huge mental confusion which might overtake him, he was taking his brother Bourguine as witness. Human relations could be simple with a little effort. Warmly, with overtones of a naked friendliness, he told him about the oven of his childhood, as somber as obscurantism itself, up to this senseless investigation which had brought him to this village, and then, by Allah and the Prophet, to the fiery love that the apparition of Yasmine and Yasmina had unleashed in his heart. When he discovered that Bourguine was their older brother he couldn't contain his joy and his candor. He told everything to his brother-in-law, absolutely everything of this conundrum, sparing no detail, be it a splinter of an idea or memory. He needed smart advice. What then, was the right choice? The whole world was tightening around him like a vise. Must he return to the valley and the police, continue to keep his peace, while cheating people? Or should he never leave the mountain, in which case he would shut the case with a slip-knot—he knew not yet how, but he would find a way, by Allah and the Prophet and all the family tie which already united us . . .

With a gloomy look Bourguine listened to his every word, followed carefully all the intricacies of his story. Then, he shuffled the cards and said:

— Cut.

They started the poker game, each winning about equally. They cheated with the same cleverness. Bourguine didn't know what to think. Willingly, he had let himself lose in order to conjure up the fate of this city man . . .

— Chief, are you quite sure we're not going the wrong way? We should have gone snooping in the North, or somewhere else, but never here. Are you sure that the capos haven't sold you a bill to pull your leg?

The chief did not answer. He was too crushed, by everything; by the heat, by the turn of events, by words.

— How could one imagine even for a second, argued the inspector, that one of these mountain people could have gotten a passport? They don't even own a decent pair of trousers like you or me.

The chief kept his silence. It was all useless, hopeless: reason, time, space.

— I beg your pardon, chief, but it's got to come out. I don't pretend that those officials are mostly crazy, aggressive or violent. No. I am simply saying, in a manner of speaking, that they have the common faults of vanity and stupidity. That they sent us here constitutes a proof, as surely as an unemployed man means somebody doesn't have a job.

The chief opened his mouth to pronounce:

— They cannot be wrong. It's mathematically impossible. You, you can be wrong. I even might be wrong. But not them. And learn once and for all that they are far from being as you say. Because, if they were stupid, they would not be where they are.

— Chief, I would like to believe in their genius. But let them try to catch a black cat, at night, in a dark room, when the cat isn't there. Where am I supposed to find a subversive among these peasants?

— The big chiefs are never wrong. You tire me. Work it out yourself.

— What do you mean by that, chief?

— Listen to me: they said that the man was here. Therefore he is here. That's all.

— But, chief . . .

— You are the one in error, I am the one who isn't reasoning properly, and those dirty asses are the ones who have something to hide. There is no other explanation.

— But, since I tell you . . .

— I don't want to hear it. Find a culprit.

— Ah? said the inspector. So that's how it's done?

— I said *a* culprit, which means: *the* culprit. There is no other.

— Ah! repeated the inspector, doubtfully.

— You would not wish, by any chance, to be stuck here forever?

— No.

— Nor would you wish to fail in the official mission that I've given you and to report a failure to the big chiefs?

— No.

— So there are no thirty-six answers. Go pick up this bastard who's making us waste time and who's upsetting me. Go do your duty. And, in fifteen days, three weeks, you'll be nominated chief. I guarantee it.

— And the file?

— What, what? What file?

— We'll have to make one, build it up with some imagination. That's the most difficult part. We'll have to type it up!

— Later, in my office. Don't think of those details now. Are you armed?

— Me? Never. I've got this, said the inspector, bursting into laughter.

— He showed his hand, fingers apart. As he left, he wondered in which way, legal or illegal, he could strangle the chief, and so well too, that even the devil himself wouldn't see through it. A mule crossed his path, head down. It was the color of the earth. For an instant, the inspector thought he recognized it. But it seemed to him that Raho's mule was red, like the flames in hell.

— Bah! he thought. It's just rolled in the dirt to shake off its fleas.

Hajja felt herself divided between the green luxuriance of her memories and the dryness of her present. This man who just spoke to her aroused in her more than mere pity: the desire to give him all. But she no longer had anything to give, not even to those to whom she had given birth. As years add to years, it had seemed to her that all around, in widening circles, the herds got smaller, the harvests were more meagre, and that a man's work was harder to find. In the olden days, the Aït Yafelman would come from the mountains, they would be day laborers, woodcutters, charcoal burners, carriers. They were paid, they would return with produce, with clothes or Turkish curly slim-toed slippers. Then, gathered around at night, there would be a big celebration, with songs and dances for the safely returned workers. Now, what do they do but wander off and stay away? Such is life; all is written. Maybe God is also a pauper now? Who knows?

These walls along which she slowly walks would have been houses in the old days. One of them had been her own house. Here, her children had been born, there they had laughed and cried, had grown. Here, there once were jars of oil and honey, and flour. Then they had to sell everything to someone she had never met: Th'state. He which had claimed what it called taxes. Maybe that was the custom of today?

Raho had told her: "Wait. Prepare for hard times." He had added: "May your soul be patient; and don't worry." He spoke little. Just the few words which removed human doubts and relieved the darkness of their existence.

They had set up a tent, but it was closed. In front of it, there was a mat on which they sat. Half a dozen women, pouring the couscous in a large round wooden plate, chattering and full of life. When Inspector Ali unceremoniously joined them, folding his sleeves and asking them to help him, their voices subsided one after another, along with their laughter and their motions. He ignored it. It was quite natural: he intimidated them! Without further ado, he broke the social barriers and got rid of the old "machismo" which reigns stupidly on Arabic soil and which confuses relations between the opposite sexes. Opposite? Who had said that? Which woman hater, ugly and impotent? Men and women were *complementary* in all things, no less! The one arousing desire in the other (and vice versa) and leading the other from stage to stage, harmoniously, to the paradise that the Koran described in an extraordinary chapter of which he barely remembered a few passages. He took a handful of the grain and tasted it. "Hmmm!" he said, his head bent to the side like a bird listening for the sounds of spring. Then he too began to stir the couscous, like a woman and with conviction, sometimes asking for a spoonful of the mixture of salt water and melted butter contained in a bowl— or better yet, for a bit of *argan* oil which would add texture to the semolina and tingle the palate. Under his agile fingers the grains were getting soaked and he sifted them, then spread them on a once white piece of cloth. Three stones were holding up an earthen pot from which he removed the lid. He tasted the boiling sauce. It was good, even delicious. It contained vegetables, lentils and even meat. He had seen them with his own eyes, those little swimming pieces of meat, the unfortunates! Of his own accord, he added a pinch of corriander, and a generous helping of *ras-al hanour*. Come what may: life was terrific.

All the while, he had not stopped moving his tongue in a flow of unrelated words (with no more connection with these women who looked at him with wide opened eyes, than with the tin cans that his own wife opened with a scraping sound which had a gift for attracting the house cat, tail in the air, and for setting human nerves on edge . . . but it was finished, thanks to God and to these two cinnamon-colored beauties!). Stirring the couscous, tasting the sauce over and over again, stirring with an olive-wood spoon, rousing the fire with his breath, he would involve any creature of the female sex who had the misfortune of answering some sally of his, then, he would continue, quite comfortable in following the inextricable maze of his thoughts. Life was life, and no doubt complex. Wasn't it man's task to simplify it? Inspector Ali had seen it all. And as civilization progressed in leaps and bounds, so life was becoming raw, acrid, hard, and unfit for human consumption. You could light a wood fire and, as long as it burned, you could see what surrounded you, you could look at your hands and feet. However, when the fire died darkness surrounded you, became a part of you. Ah! Don't ever come down, unfortunate ones! Down there, there is a darkness of words and of actions. In short, in the city only tamed animals survive. Those who have a remnant of their wild spirit are locked in zoos. Well, it's the same for humans. And he told them about it.

He told them of the opulence, without regard for truth, preferring gossip, rumors, tall tales, inter-larding a free interpretation of events. He emptied the pockets of his memory, laying out all they contained, in a jumbled pile. They were as many fluctuating notions, highly doubtful, even suspect, but which had more currency in public opinion than real facts would have had. Among the latter, a few had arrived TOP SECRET to the ears of the official, and to his sight too—and he magnified them "Africanly": they had to be matured. One had to give them all their subtler meaning in order to impress one's audience. The word was the word since the Hegira. Why then stop in mid course? Why not let the living word ride at full speed? Were one to pull in one's mount, one would risk ending up astride a rocking horse.

By Allah and the Prophet, those stories he told were salty, and peppered to taste. He could see that his audience was bashfully turning its head and modestly lowering its eyes; but he couldn't care less. For him, all truth had to be whole, complete with all its limbs, like Adam and Eve's son, two eyes, two ears, and a mouth. Only when she was sweetened, did truth become deaf, dumb, and blind. Simple truth is lifeless. Just like one of those TV shows, but thank God you don't even know what TV is! Extrapolating, embellishing, imitating various TV personalities, raising laughter (his own was the first to burst out), he was a memorable story teller in this late afternoon, a true wise man who carried the day. In this exercise he learned haphazardly, in spite of himself, because his ears functioned independently from his body, that this peasant woman in front of him, who looked at him sharply from under the straw hat gnawed at the rim, was called Lalla, that she was the mother of Yasmine and Yasmina, and thus his mother-in-law *illico presto;* that this other one, who was wiping her eyes with her apron and who poked him, cry-ing: "Stop! stop! Ah! dear man, enough!" was Zineb, who could be his aunt by marriage, no less; and this skinny young girl who hadn't laughed, because she was deaf, was his cousin, although, perhaps, she was a niece five times removed . . . . A whole family with roots like cedar, underground as well as above, drawing their sap from the centuries gone by. Would one, by any chance be connected with his family line? Struck by this sudden idea, he told them of his own family, dead and buried by now, and may Allah keep their souls in peace! May they not fidget in their graves, for their own sake. Ah! if only they knew! . . . . In great detail, he described them and brought them to life. He himself expected to see his father blowing on the fire and his mother placing the couscous container on the flame and making little holes in the bubbling skin to allow the aromatic steam to escape from the broth. That's what was done back when there was still a semblance of genuine couscous . . .

When he stopped talking, his throat was dry, his liver gorged with his feelings. And he stopped because he had run out of words, and because he was nagged by the remembrance, distant and confused though it was, of a certain inquest. He got up, arms dangling, more orphaned than ever, on the far side of the twentieth century. When he had first joined these women to chat briefly of his past, they had timidly welcomed him. He now was leaving them—happy with them, and himself: their ideas were much the same, just as the official statements of the government had declared. Now what? Where further might he go with his nostalgia and his joy? One served so well as a crutch to the other, over the years . . .

The first drum beat resounded at that moment, at the very instant when inspector Ali started up the path leading to the cave. Pulsing, heavy, slow, it echoed off the rocks. Another beat answered it, coming from the lower mountain ranges; then others boomed in between heaven and the mountain. Incessantly the vibrations wove into space and time like the ferment-soaked voice of recaptured solitude.

"Wake up, hey!" the inspector said to himself. "It's only the orchestra rehearsing for tonight. Hajja told me about it. Don't go imagining worse."

Yet, he could hardly fail to feel the profound and "earthy" inflections that moved him so strongly. Where, and in what former life had he heard them?

"Don't be afraid, Ali," he told himself. "It's only the drums. Those peasants play outdoors, not in up-to-date recording studios. That's why you strain your ear with surprise. Better yet, don't forget couscous is cooking, so be glad!"

Then, the piercing sound of a desert flute arose suddenly, silvering the drum beats like a long tear. Then, the sound was gone, in the space of a birth—or death. When it came once again, it was endless, spreading from eternity to eternity, across the horizon, modulating in quarter tones, restating sound and sense on another octave with the same *esprit.* Another reed flute joined in, and then many others, like a chorus of hill wolves. "That concert," Ali thought, "I know it too, I've heard it before." Shuddering and, without realizing it, he hastened his steps.

"It's only reed flutes, nothing to worry about," he told himself. "Only some mountain people from the Middle Ages, singing their happiness to live in the hereafter. You're not afraid of a mere stem of reed?" he challenged himself. "Isn't the hereafter that the Koran describes as beautiful? Well, then? Allah did say: 'We will gather your bones no matter where you may be; we will revive you . . . . We are closer to you than your own jugular . . .'"

He had almost reached his goal. Just twenty meters more . . . only six steps. He would enter the cave, with his decision, work it out in a few words with his ex-chief, throw back at him his instructions, then tear them into four, then eight, then thirty-two pieces. He wouldn't get close to this investigation, either with the police or with the state.

— Well, maybe, I won't do any such thing. Scream, sure, that's true. I'll shout, but that's all. I laugh because I have to. And lots of talk, too much of it . . .but that's all I ever do . . ."

So he babbled on internally in quiet desperation. For he knew that he had lost all true identity, that he was a mere clerk, a straw man. Caught body and soul in the huge mechanism of the state, he had become incapable of any action other than arresting and manhandling people, just to survive. He slowed down, then stopped.

Why did he come to think of a blind man when he turned his gaze to catch a last flash of the splendor of the setting sun? If the sun were unknown to a blind man except for its heat and what he could imagine (a black sun), so the earth should be unknown to him. And that was for the best ... yes, for the best! ...

— The blind, he whispered suddenly. There was one of them here yesterday.

He suddenly recalled the man's name: Basfao. And, all at once insignificant details came to life in his mind: a red mule dawdling, turned dust color; Hajja, who had lost, in just a day, her musical laughter; remembering her tears and her pain when he had asked her for her eternal hospitality; Bourguine saying, "cut"; the grave that Raho was digging; his spade, and his caustic look . . . . A whole spider's web, an enormous web that these primitives had woven to catch the representatives of this end of the twentieth century. It all made sense! Ah, and that accompaniment of reed flutes also made sense, those drums resounding from the depths of the ages; they, too, had a terrifying significance . . .

Inspector Ali catapulted himself toward the cave's entrance . . . he must arm himself.

The tip of a horn-handled knife nudged him in the chest and, from the void, came Bourguine's voice:

— Aji, my brother. Come. Raho wants to see you.

No, it was no use trying to move. It would have been impossible to do so anyway: his arms had already been immobilized by half a dozen peasants. His legs, too. No, oh no, it was no use wondering what had happened to the chief. Even more useless to attempt to look into the cave.

— Aji, my brother! concluded Bourguine.

From east to west the flutes modulated their hymn to the dead while the drum beat throbbed with intercession, petitioning in their grave voices the forgiveness of God and man.

134

10

A shovel, straight up, the handle pointing to the sky. The sharp point of a pick axe plunged into the gaping tomb, as if the instrument were ready to go into action to dig the hole. All around were the piles of earth and stones. Behind the trench a skin tent. At the opening to the tent, seated on his heels, Raho. Piney torches lighted up his face with coppery reflections. He spoke:

— I am not your judge.

And he was quiet. He spoke:

— It will be the council that will decide. All of us. We are one and the same family.

From the *djebels* to the village square no one added a word. Everybody waited, in small, compact groups, the Ait Yafelman, the mountaineers having come in from places all around. Only the sound of flutes had never ceased and the drums rumbling low out in back like an echo. Their tempo had the slow patience of obstination. Raho lifted his hand and they died away. He said:

— Take the skin and bury your comrade. He is dead. Tomorrow it will be hot.

Then the tambours, heavy, grave, struck up again asking Allah to pardon the sins of this man who had come to die. Ali was not bound. No one was constraining him. He was free in his movements, but he was smart enough instinctively to know that the single danger would have been in seeking to flee. He didn't throw another look at the oblong pile covered by a tarpaulin from which nothing could be seen except a pair of boots. He said, weeping with hot tears:

— Oh, that Allah rest his soul there where it is!

He began to stammer:

— You . . . you . . .

He cried while the tambours rumbled even more quietly as if they were no more than a murmur of pardon:

— Oh, what fools you are! You imagined perhaps that *they* will not come to know. But *they* will know and *they* will come to avenge him! Ah! By Allah and the Prophet, one can see that you've never got out of your hole in the Middle Ages! Listen! Listen now! From the hair of the governor, without forgetting the waiters in the cafés and the cops, *they* have made his country their personal business. This jerk of a chief was one of theirs!

Without even lifting his voice, without even giving his words the least tone of a command, Raho said:

— Place your friend in the hole and cover him with rocks and earth.

He added:

— The grave has been dug east to west. Put his head in the direction of Mecca. He was a Muslim in his infancy.

Storming into this quiet voice was a shout like a bird of prey:

— Your turn will come.

The rumbling of the tambours died down to give way to the sound of flutes. Ali, shivering at the sound of this musical plaint, knew that he had to shush it immediately, before anything. As long as one drum was speaking he had a chance. But now that the flutes were rising up sovereign the silhouettes became agitated, indistinct phrases and broken sounds washed over his ears. What was it that his mother had spoken of long ago, what obscure forces were coming from the ancient times? At the beginning of the world, she had said (slowly, there, way back in his childhood, there huddled in the hovels, while her husband baked the bread of others), way before religions and the civilizations of the State, there had been a terrestrial life for men. "Yes," she had said, "really a long time ago, before time, the world had been for mankind. It was a veritable paradise. There never has been another. And the sky; it was unknown. It was from there that the danger came. The wind, meteors, the drought and the deluge, calamities. That was what our ancestors had, before they lost the memory of it and began to believe the legends which had come down from the sky. The old ones asserted that life here below had been without malady, without hate or death. Before History, there were plants and milk in abundance and fields of cereals without number and all the fruits of the nourishing earth. But, there above, was the sky and its savage population, the gods. They were jealous, envious. From their stars, they cast down death on the human race. One of them, a long, long time ago, even tried to charm them with his devilish instrument, a flute. He was called Bann*, I believe. This is what they narrated in the olden days, before the astrals claimed that it was all dreams and lies and that which we had been told by our ancestors as being true only existed in books. But my mother spoke to me of the beginning of the world and it was my grandmother who had told it to my mother—and so from generation to generation going all the way back in time. There's no

*The god Pan

reason to repudiate this memory; we must not succumb to the legends of our enemies. Because they came down among us to . . ."

— Leave off this idle talk, Ali, he said to himself with fear and anger.

Ah, how heavy were the breathings enclosing him. Smoky torches, flickering. And the earth upon which he would fall down sooner or later. And cold testimony, metallic, unpitying, was the sky. The flute broke in again to push him up against his terror, despite himself, despite his soul bolted to his body, because it was there, the terror, more actual than life itself. Not to die, but to die for nothing. Without reflecting, by instinct, he spoke to Raho, stepping toward him right up to the edge of the grave which separated them, saying:

— *Bismillahi rahmani rahim!*

— Yes, approved Raho; in the name of Allah all forgiveness and mercy. And then?

— You promised me . . . my rifle . . . you . . .

— Yes, said Raho.

— You promised to give it to me this evening. You said it would be evening.

— Yes, said Raho. I promised.

Raho took a moment to reflect, all the time he could to listen to his bones and to reach down even into their marrow, the elements of a life. And when he began to speak as the song of the flutes quieted and amid the muffled beating of the drums, there came a far away voice, almost as if it weren't there.

— It was a man of our group, my grandson. He was called Basfao. At first he lived here. And then, he went down there below, to the other side of the mountain, in the country of the Algerians. He couldn't see too well, that's true. He worked there for many years in a fertilizer factory. I don't know what there is in that substance, but he was blinded. Then he returned to us. That was the man that you had come to hunt out with your automobile, your police, your weapons. And I know well that, if you had found him, that would have been the hour that he would have been cast into one of your prisons. There, there's your gun! It's loaded, it doesn't lack a single cartridge.

He reached around behind him grabbing the weapon with both hands. He threw it up over his head. Ali caught it in full flight, opened the magazine, expelling the cartridges which fell at his feet, and then cast the weapon away as if it were a filthy object. Through the rumbling of the drums and the murmurs which quickly rose, he was able to hear the voice of hope: that of Bourguine who was standing at his side: "This is a brother"; the kind voice of Hajja: "The evil is not in him; he doesn't know what he has done, but the evil is not truly in him"; there were others also who admired his courage . . . and dominating everything, the voice of his mother, coming from the past and continuing her ancient story: "They had always lusted after the earth. Consumed by gluttony, they had exhausted the stars. They had even burned the

137

moon and the sun. And their sky had become empty, without life. Then they fell down amongst us. They wanted our paradise and ourselves as their slaves. Oh! They were tricky, those gods! More intelligent than we would ever be. Their power came from their hearts and their brains. They reinforced themselves with what they called the law, from books which they forced us to read: the book of Hebrews, those of the Christians, the Koran of the Islamic ones . . . huge numbers of others which they pretended were holy and sacred. And it was in that way that they arranged the ordering of things and put lies in the place of truth. They even divided terrestrial life in two parts; that which came to be called the Good and that which came to be called the Evil. And so our ancestors and their descendants began to battle with their own bodies and to believe that the sky held true paradise and that the earth, our nourishing mother, was hell. Some of us had refused to convert to the religion of the gods and fled, but not many. The majority succumbed to these unspeakable things. And thus it was that they began to work for their masters like slaves and to construct buildings and cities and to create machines and more machines of which they had no need. And their descendants continued more and more with ever greater grief to believe in nothingness. And that will never end. Because the gods have boiled our heads, they have mixed their language of lies and magic in ours, they have rubbed out our memory of the ancient days. And so it is that we are now divided, brothers from brothers, and our own words contradict the words of the tribe. And they made us spill the blood of animals, then our own blood, to be worthy of the hell of the sky which they call paradise. Oh! They are terribly clever, terribly persuasive. They have sold sand to the Taureg and have made them believe who knows what. They are of such a sort that mankind on this earth can no longer ever be content with his lot. And, when they perceived that their books were worn out like old figs and that they couldn't get anything from them or next to nothing, then they invented another stratagem: progress, civilization. Here and there, in the plain and down in other countries and far off in the most distant lands, it it above all the same civilization. But the gods divided them by giving them different physiognomies and placing different languages in their mouths. And then, the descendants of the people of the earth were even more divided . . ."

— You are of the 20th century, Ali, don't concern yourself with these phantom thoughts. Wake up, quick! Quick! they're nothing but the chimeras of the old woman of the legends who talks about the ancient days. Wake up in this world and look around. Think quickly and act. Speak to Raho. He's the only one you really have to convince. Engage him, speak to him in his own language, don't have any fear, get on with it. He's looking at you. Everbody's staring at you.

Fear still dominated him (the oldest thing, the most ancient) though he forced himself to speak:

— I didn't know anything, neither that he had worked with our brothers, the Algerians, nor that someone was looking for him for whatever reason. It was the chief who had everything in his head, and now he is dead. So, how can I be a witness to things of which I was the most ignorant?

He followed it up, vehemently, spinning on his heels to face all four cardinal points, disregarding whatever danger there might be from the earth or the sky, but it was always Raho to whom he addressed the end of his phrases:

— It's only been two hours, perhaps three, but I don't have any notion of time despite the watches of civilization . . . just two or three hours of the clock ago that I learned from his mouth (so full of perplexities and foolishnesses!) what we were after. I tell you! Nothing but bribes . . . ah! You don't know these chiefs. They keep everything to themselves. Even secret thoughts. And this one was the most miserly of all, but he is dead now. Allah rest his soul where it is, and he will no longer come to haunt my days and nights! Except for that, I would have become insane for good. Who was I, me, eh? A servant, a vartlet, nothing more. "Ali, hand me my shirt, dirty offspring of your mother . . . Ali, note what I am going to say to you, listen carefully, crocodile head . . . " It's all very simple; there I was in my bed, sleeping peacefully. I didn't even know of the existence of this village or its inhabitants. I tell the truth. And when I learned what the chief proposed to do, I began sorting things out in my head, by Allah and the Prophet! Good, is he dead? He is dead. Consequently, he will never know, the poor guy, what I was planning to do behind his back. He always took me for a big imbecile.

— And what was it that you worked out in your head? interrupted a strong voice. Speak out.

— By Allah and the Prophet, here's what I was going to do: return with him to town and set the machinery going to fill out the police records and orders. I had plenty of files on him, isn't that true? I wasn't at all mixed up on that point. I would have said to them: "The true criminal, the subversive you are looking for, even up in the mountains, well, it's he, he the chief." Ah, that hits you, eh? Now, how much of what I say would these types accept? I can't say exactly, but this is the sort of thing that happens frequently. I tell you, once you get above a certain rank, you begin to regard the chiefs with a cynical eye, especially when they grab power for themselves. That's when you look at them with a jaundiced eye. Each is scrutinizing the other, you know what I mean?

The crowd murmured. And now it was grumbling without restraint, blocking out the voices of the flutes and the drums.

— He lies.

— He's telling outrageous stories.

— He's all mixed up, muttered Hajja. He doesn't really know what he's saying . . . his words are all scrambled up.

— He's taking us for jackasses.

— Let him speak, ordered Raho. The night will be long.

Ali wagged his tongue all through the night, manipulating reason so well as to transform it into pure and simple irreason. All the way to dawn . . .

(. . . *How can we give ease to the ancient folk? We, here in the cities, your*

139

father, members of the family, we can but disguise our souls while waiting for hope, it's not necessary that they know that we are against them. For centuries, those of us who have never had the chance to flee have had to pretend to adopt their customs and their laws . . . and to venerate them. And thus, the gods and their servants have left us a little in peace. Impoverished, raped of the products of our soil, but at peace. They don't know what remains deep down inside of us. If they were to realize, they would put us to death—or, even worse, they would exterminate our very souls, just as they did to those of our ancestors. So, we act like idiots, we behave like savages, as ignorant and inferior dolts in order to disarm them. That's what we all must absolutely do if we wish to survive at all. Some of us come, with the passage of time, to forget what they really are. This sort is happy in a way with what they are . . . c'est la vie . . . Nothing else, I well believe. Some little groups in the hills or the desert, others hidden away in the impenetrable jungles. These have never ceased taking flight as the conquerors have marched in with their legions and slaves. That's what my mother told me, the stuff she heard from her mother, and so on, from generation to generation, climbing through the centuries. It seems that they survive still, despite the gods and their innumerable servitors who have become even worse than their masters. They collect during the full moon and recall the bygone days and beat their drums and tom-toms. One of them plays a flute in order to remind them of death which forever lies in wait, so that they may keep on guard. But, it's always the drums which win out. To this very time . . . right up to now . . . because one day, they will die: they won't have the wherewithal even to subsist. Then . . . that's when the savage peoples shall have exhausted the earth as well, having destroyed it as they did their stars, long long ago, before time began . . .)

Right up to dawn, he said everything, did everything, was everything, with an all-embracing sincerity. The hardest had pierced the head of Raho and forced him to admit that, well, he had not betrayed the laws of hospitality; that though appearances were against him—with the weight of tribal law, ah, well, in such a case he was prepared to die, without further ado, once and for al. The rifle was there, he had but to pick up the cartridges and load it. Or the knife with the horn handle which had proved itself in Algeria and which had inflicted the chief with his handsome death, or that pickaxe which had no task in the grave, no matter how blunt or sharp an instrument. He summoned up words and phrases which he himself did not understand, nor would he ever . . .

Raho remained obstinately simple, slow and patient: for him, a son of Eve and of Adam, who had requested the hospitality in Allah's name, could engage his soul to behave with honor. He would not yield from that.

— Honor? cried out Ali. Where is there any place for honor in the institutions of civilization today? Even in the countries of the Christians, and in the homeland of *L'amerikanes*? Let me explain it . . .

Tenacious, he explained to them that he, looking like an Arab, and a complete Muslim living in town, he had become a dog in the course of years in almost all respects: his tasks, his relationships, even his kennel ration . . . A hound dumb to any sense of honor, inevitably. But, after just one day and one night passed in this village among the Ait Yafelman, he had come to realize the vanity, the stupidity of his prior life. He had decided to abandon all of that former existence so as to live with his brothers of the mountains, isn't that so, Hajja? . . . And Hajja supported his moving "witness' word for word, telling what Ali had indeed spoken to her, and what she had said to him in return, adding that he was but a poor orphan abandoned by Allah and man and that he believed himself intelligent, but that she pardoned him and had confidence in him despite all. Ali heard her out with great respect, tears formed in his eyes and a dark anger swelled up in his heart against himself. He shook hands with the old woman, turning then to a drummer making the instrument resonate in the ritualistic rhythm.

— I am like you, he concluded. A poor sort lost in civilization and enmeshed in the "copishness" of civilization.

Raho had attended earnestly to what he had said. He now spoke out in a tone of destiny:

— Before dawn comes, if the council so decides, there will be no trace of you nor of your colleague, nor of your baggage, nor of your automobile. Nothing.

Here Ali made his final effort. He sought to prove to him and to the rest that such a course would be the greatest error of their lives, since there were records at Headquarters, and he went around from group to group with his incessant words, springing, energetic, here, there, everywhere. Ah, yes, agreed, they could dismantle the old buggy into bits and pieces to sell them all over the Sudan, indeed a fine solution. And of course they could dump the corpses, his and the chief's, into a hole in hell. Oh yes, yes, by Allah! But how would they suppress the papers at Headquarters, down there, in the capital of the cops and the government? The documents, the commands setting up this mission, had an enduring life . . .

Do what you wish, men of the council. Ah! Very good! You can do what you want in your wisdom of wise men of this and surrounding villages. And within three days, in a week at the outside, it won't be a matter of two suckers like us to worry about . . . because I have to let you have it, I have the courage to tell you: locked into his chiefly pride, the chief thought you were but clods, furnished merely with sheep's brains, good-for-nothings whom he could lead about by the nose just by flashing his uniform at you, the bloody ass. Allah rest his soul wherever it is, among the millions and millions of asses who have bossed this earth. Ah, and that's not all! By Allah and the Prophet, the government naturally will send you machine guns and bombing planes . . . Do what you wish. Me, I give up.

He acted out the cataclysm of machine guns firing, and the bombs falling, exploding . . . mimicking the crash of falling walls, the shuddering of the mountain like a giant volcano. And then he sat down. He now had no force left to contemplate any further fate, even a day or two. Perchance he dreamt of what would arrive: two *houris** of paradise at his side, night and morn and especially throughout the night—on to the end of all time, they always would be so beautiful, never aging. What did they used to call them? . . . His mother had unwound the tales of waking sleep, oh, with what persuasive power! For a bit one had to believe in them, he, the ancient wolf, the lonely stalker always and everlastingly in battle against life. His brains had capsized, that was it. He ended by dozing off . . .

Someone shook him, lifting him to his feet, then pulling him into the tent. The drums no longer rattled, and quiet were the flutes. Alone, a score of men had stayed out the night, torch-lit. They circled him—a solid ring. They addressed him again and again, leaving him not a moment of rest. How would he carry out his sabotage of the government papers? What solution did he propose? No, that wouldn't work, his comrade's corpse ought to be buried in this place, that was the custom. Ali battled word for word with them, argument against argument, sometimes spreading out to the entire assembly, because they at times all spoke at once, and he had to rethread their arguments in order to oppose them. He, the joker in life, so much the fantacist in daily

*Islamic maidens of Heaven

142

speech (and in his head), he knew the kind of person that they expected him to be, solemn, thoughtful, efficient. A true capo.

So he went on with his elaborate menu, hitting all the notes necessary to chime in with the level of comprehension of his interrogators, who, not really, no, that wasn't the thing to do—instead it was better to place the mortal remains of the chief on the back-seat of the car . . . No, he had no idea if this fellow had friends or family, but that wasn't the question. Dead or alive, this

man had to be returned to his true family, the police: or the State, if you wish . . . The police had usurped everything, even his soul. That was clear, as surely as four and three make . . . How could he go to extinguish the blaze and calm the situation so that not an arrow would light on the village, let alone bombs? O.K., you who can't read, I am going to do so, listen. Here is what I write up: *primo*, the big-shots are always right; they always see most clearly; there was indeed a subversive, a dangerous criminal in this peaceable village, that never had any bad record. (You shouldn't get worried about that, I'll invent the guy's name, gving chapter and verse with all the convincing details, stuffing the report with pages and pages: they love that stuff . . .) *Segundo*: I'll write how Chief Mohammed was just about to collar the guy when a big battle broke out. My regretted chief and friend fell mortally from many slashes of a knife (oh, just one, you say?) and the bloody bastard who did it took off for Algeria. You all tried to hunt him down, I'll say, all of you here, and I, myself. What they do about it, they'll have to work out amongst themselves, seeing it as a diplomatic incident . . . But there'll have to be evidence. Written proofs.

At dawn, Ali had survived the long inquest. Raho and the young man of the glasses knew how to sign their names and they did so with some difficulty. Three or four of the men drew stars. The rest of the Ait Yafelman had to be satisfied with giving up their thumbprints.

The noise of the motor died out at the horizon—and the sun rose with a new day. Raho and Hajja, seated face to face, were alone on the mountain-side.

— You didn't believe him, really? questioned Hajja.

— No.

— But you let him save his skin.

— His hour had not yet come.

He stared off in the silence, eyes wet and luminous. Then he spoke:

— They know now who we are. I have to think about it a bit.

Hajja kissed him on the forehead and rose. As always, she had a deep faith that he knew what he was doing.

144

11

    Chief of Police Ali arrived at the village one September dawn. Between the great plateaus and the lower shoulders of the Atlas Mountains, shimmering in the emerald light, suffused with turquoise and rubies, roared a circling helicopter.

The chief was driving a Land Rover furnished with a radio transmitter. He was on an official visit and he was leading it openly. Above him, there ranked a pyramid of chiefs, unknown to him for the most part—not even by name. And, orders were orders. Up and down the hierarchical ladder, the rungs descended to him, in the form of impersonal notes scribbled in red pencil and followed by illegible signatures. But Chief Ali felt obliged to react only to those stamped with the official seal, the imperial eagle. He was the opposite of an irresponsible sort or a cretin.

Halting the vehicle in the little stony place of the village, switching off the ignition, giving a sigh, lighting up a cigar, he gave a sharp poke with his elbow to his traveling companion, Inspector Smaïl, whose head rested peacefully on the dashboard.

— Wake up! he shouted.

Inspector Smaïl pulled himself together, then turning two eyes full of sand on his chief, he gasped:

— I wasn't sleeping, chief. I was thinking.

— Ah, responded the chief. You were thinking? Ah, very well, Inspector Smaïl, but no one asks you to do that. Moreover, now's not the time. Open the door, get out, and get the submachine guns ready.

Until the fall of night they stalked around the village, cave by cave, and all around. A void. Not a soul.

February 18, 1981

146